LILY FARRELL

JUST CAN'T GET ENOUGH

HARKER
HOUSE

Cover design by Violet Fenn

First edition

ISBN: 978-1-7395926-0-8

This book was professionally typeset on Reedsy.
Find out more at reedsy.com

dancing through the living room entirely naked, if it happened to coincide with the F1 motor racing being on television.

But I could say one thing for Dan—he wasn't in the habit of disappearing out of my life the way Marc Gatton had. Marc had been through a well-documented fight with pretty much every addiction in the book, before having a very public breakdown. Drink, drugs, sex—you name it, he'd done it to excess. For a good couple of years the only photographs of him that appeared in the press were under lurid headlines that wondered how much longer he could go on living like this. The answer was 'not very'—the police picked him up after they found him off his head and alone in the gutter of a London backstreet, before being dumped unceremoniously into rehab. After that, he just...disappeared. The rest of Black Swans—the band he'd formed in his teens with his best friend Paul Fisher; the band that had somehow dominated the charts whilst also being loved by critics—never spoke about him publicly, all of them bound either by astounding loyalty or cast-iron NDAs. I was sad, briefly. But a long time had passed since our midnight conversations—me under the duvet, him smiling glossily out from the secondhand music magazines I searched for online and avidly bought at any mention of him, even well into my twenties—and adult Jem wasn't quite so impressed by his excesses as hormonal teenage Jem might have been. But now, years later, Black Swans had reappeared. A small tour had been announced with great fanfare and the original band had started doing publicity with vaguely confused expressions on their faces, as if *they* couldn't quite believe it, either. A warm up gig had been booked in the town hall of the suburb where I lived with Dan. Most of the inevitable gossip revolved around why on earth a band as big as Black Swans had decided to restart their careers in a tiny suburban theatre.

"I reckon they're not entirely convinced that he'll manage it," Zoe had sniffed when I told her. Zoe Hayward was the most cynical person I knew, led a hair-raising life as a writer for *The Gossip*—one of the marginally less trashy weekly women's magazines—and had been my best friend since childhood. She'd started work as a filing clerk at a fashion magazine the day after we left sixth form and had been the Gossip's resident lifestyle columnist (aka the 'any scurrilous rumours she could get away with without being sued for libel' column) for the past five years. People often seemed surprised that we were still so close despite having such different lifestyles, but we needed each other for balance and we both knew it. I occasionally needed reminding that there was an exciting world outside of my safe and steady life and Zoe had actually said out loud on more than one occasion that she liked having someone around who'd known her forever and wasn't easily impressed by her lifestyle. Things weren't quite as glamorous as they seemed, anyway—Zoe actually earned very little money and lived in the attic room of her elderly great-aunt's house in Tottenham. Luckily for her, Aunt Sophie was not only a very broadminded child of the sixties, she was also extremely deaf—both of which were helpful when Zoe dragged her endless conquests home in the early hours or decided to hold a party in her large but stuffy loft space. I'd once been queueing for the loo on the middle floor when Sophie had appeared on the stairwell, wondering what where the noise was coming from. She'd taken in the sight of several complete strangers in fancy dress hanging around outside her bathroom with nothing more than a brief, "Aah, you kids have fun, now," before giggling her way back down the stairs.

Zoe and I met up for coffee most weeks and she tried to persuade me into working with her every single time, reminding me of the fun events and free lunches I was missing out on. And every time I pointed out that I could live without writing hungover copy about second rate television actors whilst resentfully drinking some concoction that—the beauty desk insisted—would stop my skin ageing and was probably made with unicorn piss. I didn't have an issue with the magazine itself; it was more that everyone involved appeared to hate each other with barely suppressed passion. No wonder there was such a high rate of nervous breakdowns and diazepam addictions in Zoe's office. But I did sometimes secretly wonder whether I might have more fun if my levels of unicorn piss were higher.

Whatever the motives behind the unexpected Black Swans gig, it was a big deal for Uppingwood. Arthur Blackwell, the Mercury's editor-in-chief and old friend of my father, had personally asked me to cover it for them. One of the last surviving old-school local newspapers, the Mercury had fought off three separate takeover attempts in the last five years alone, somehow managing to cling to its out-of-date traditions even as equivalent publications across the country were being absorbed into increasingly powerful media companies. I strongly suspected that this was entirely down to the tenacity of its long-term boss and that the vultures would be circling within minutes of his eventual retirement. This, of course, was precisely why Arthur *didn't* retire. He might have been a stubborn old mule and old-fashioned in his ways, but he was kindly and solid and I liked him. Asking me to cover the gig wasn't as flattering as it sounded, mind. I'd got the job by default, the rest of the Mercury's staff being either old enough to have no idea who Black Swans were or staid enough not to care. The only one who might possibly have been interested in Marc's antics was Tristan, the Mercury's receptionist, who loved a bad boy and insisted on telling me all about his inevitably disastrous encounters with them in mortifyingly regular detail.

"I'm going to head into the office," said Dan, sitting up. "Want the bathroom first?" He clambered out of bed and headed for the bathroom without waiting for an answer, his gingery-blond hair stuck flat to his head. "I probably won't see you tonight," this was news to me, "I'm going out for a drink with the lads. Thought we'd head into town for a bit." When you lived where we did, 'into town' meant central London. Tucked away in the far reaches of the northeast London suburbs, Uppingwood might look like the sort of town in which Miss Marple could have happily solved her mysteries, but it was still somehow clinging on to the London transport network. This meant that Dan would inevitably stagger home in the early hours, having slept most of the way back on the night bus. I heard metallic clanking as he turned the water on for the shower. The ominous creaking noise of the hot water slowly heading through the ancient metal pipes did nothing to disguise the sound of my beloved ripping a thunderous fart on the other side of the closed door. I sighed and got out of bed. Deciding that life would probably be a tiny bit nicer if I didn't wait to use the bathroom after Lord Fartpants, I just squirted some deodorant on and got dressed. The Mercury was a leisurely walk from my flat and I had to walk past a Greggs—I'd just pick up coffee and a slab of cake on the way. Picking up my bag from the coffee table, I headed towards the door, shouting goodbye as I went. I wasn't sure whether I could be heard over the tuneless singing emanating from the shower, but I doubted it mattered.

"Are you with us, Jem?" Arthur slapped my desk with his copy of *The Racing Post*. My eyes snapped open to find him staring down at me with a faintly bemused expression on his face. Shit. I crossed invisible fingers that my brief daydream—Marc again, this time *sans* trousers, because why the hell shouldn't I have imaginary fun if I wasn't getting any in reality—hadn't included any audio. Arthur shook his head. "I do hope you'll be able to hold a coherent conversation with this chap," he fretted, sweat stains visible in the armpits of his neatly pressed shirt. Mrs Blackwell would be horrified. She was fastidious about her husband's appearance, believing that the editor of the local weekly paper was on a par with being the town mayor. In a place like Uppingwood, she probably wasn't far wrong. The Mercury covered everything from flower shows to traffic issues and was mostly staffed through nepotism rather than merit. My 2:1 in English was less important than my dad having been in the army with my boss several decades earlier. Arthur veered between inadvertent sexism—sending me to cover WI meetings, asking when I was going to put the kettle on—and enthusiastically pushing me as the Mercury's 'voice of the youth'. The fact that I'd turned thirty a few months earlier made no difference, because the only person younger than me in the office was Tristan. And he hadn't been allowed to take on anything more taxing than reception and filing duties since that time he seduced the headmaster of the local comprehensive when he was supposed to be reporting on their excellent exam results. The man himself was hovering in the doorway, waiting for Arthur to leave so that he could perch on the edge of my desk and gossip. Gossiping was Tris's passion—that and bitching about reality television, which he seemed to watch an awful lot of, considering he claimed to hate it. Arthur gave one last loud sigh and sweated his way back to his corner office, where he would no doubt smoke a cigar out of the window in defiance of all health and safety regulations and spend the afternoon sneakily watching the horse racing on his laptop. Tris immediately scuttled over.

"So, what's the plan of action, Jemimah?" he asked, perching on my desk and waggling his eyebrows dramatically. "Interviewing the teen dream, are we? Been kissing your posters in preparation?" I glared at him.

"It's a long time since Marc Gatton's even been famous, let alone pinned to my bedroom wall," I said, sourly.

"I bet you'd like him to pin *you* to the wall though," sniggered Tristan. "You know I'd be your wingman, only I've got a hot date with Simon from accounts. I'm sure you're perfectly capable of controlling yourself without an escort." He didn't look convinced. I gave up pretending.

"Oh fucking *hell*, Tris," I wailed, "how am I going to interview Marc bloody Gatton without making a complete arse of myself?" I glared at the distorted reflection in the computer screen in front of me. My scraggy blonde hair stuck out all over the place and I cursed at myself for not having had my roots done recently. The disappointing reflection of my own face was blurred over the email from Mike Goldren, manager of Black Swans, agreeing to their interview with the Mercury. It was a mark of Marc's fall from grace that he was even doing it—it wasn't very long ago that he was wanted by all of the papers, but refused to speak to any of them. Tris was gazing at me thoughtfully, his head tipped to one side.

"You know, Jem, you could scrub up really nice if you tried." I bristled, but he ploughed on. "Why don't I come over to yours before you head off out tonight and give you a bit of a makeover?" He grinned at me. "There's nothing in that ancient body and brain of your that couldn't be fixed with a bit of effort." I cut him off before he could embarrass either of us any further.

"Tristan, you are so creepy sometimes." He shrugged and didn't bother to deny it. "I'm going as I am. Marc Gatton can take me as he finds me." *Although I definitely wish he would just take me,* said a traitorous voice in my head.

YEAH, BUT HE'S DROP DEAD GORGEOUS

Having finally managed to convince Tris that yes, I would put some makeup on and at least brush my hair before the gig, I headed home down the road that ran alongside the park. When I got to my street, I counted the houses as I walked, something I'd done for years. *One, two, three…*I muttered to myself until I came to number seven. Lucky for some. My street was unusual in that the house numbers went all the way up one side then back down the others, rather than having odds and evens on separate sides. Heading through the gate, I nodded hello to Mrs Jarvis at number ten. We lived close enough to know each other by name, but far enough apart not to be expected to hold a proper conversation. This suited me just fine. I rooted around in my bag for my house keys and, having found them underneath a packet of tissues, old cinema tickets and a tatty, single condom packet that I vaguely remembered Zoe forcing on me several years previously—*'Always better to be prepared!'* she'd said at the time—I let myself in. My front door would have originally been the side entrance to the house, before it had been split into two flats at some point during the 1960s. The couple who lived downstairs were earnest vegans who home educated their kids and tried—with varying levels of success—to be self-sufficient. The back garden was technically mine, but not long after they'd moved in a few years previously, Sid and Nancy (they were genuinely called that—it had caused me great amusement when they first told me, but they didn't seem to get the joke) had asked if I'd consider swapping. Dad hadn't been convinced—"You're lowering the value of the property, love," he'd warned me—so in the end I'd told them to just use mine as well as their own. It saved me bothering with maintenance and I'd often come home to find random vegetables wrapped in newspaper on my doorstep. No plastic bags for Sid and Nancy. I admired their tenacity, especially as neither of their kids seemed in the slightest bit grateful for the amazing start in life that their parents were offering them. A pair of boy/girl pre-teen twins, they spent most of their time shouting at each other and loudly refusing to join in with the various hale and hearty activities that their parents thought up. I let myself in and bent to collect the post from the doormat. Today's exciting mail consisted of a free advertising paper and a copy of a local charity magazine who'd added me to their mailing list without permission after I'd written an article about them six months previously. Dumping my bag on the coffee table, I went into the bathroom and started the shower running so that it would warm up whilst I rooted for something to wear to watch the man of my dreams leap around on stage right in front of me. Just the thought of it made me feel sick with nerves. Maybe he would look ancient and thoroughly past-it in reality, I thought almost hopefully. Although it would be disappointing, it would definitely make interviewing him easier afterwards.

An hour before the gig was due to start, I was glaring at my reflection in the bathroom mirror. Dan had left the window open when he'd gone to work and although the entire flat was now freezing cold, it had at least allowed the bathroom to air out. I'd never have admitted it to Tris, but I definitely took more care with my appearance than usual, pinning up my hair to disguise the roots and applying more eyeliner than I'd worn in years. Rather inexpertly, I belatedly realised, peering closer and scrutinising my smudgy work. Hopefully the panda-eyed look was still in fashion. Not that I'd ever been one to follow fashion, despite Zoe's endless attempts to educate me (including an ill-advised appearance in the Gossip's regular makeover section, which people still ribbed me about years later). I ended up wearing a clean version of exactly the same outfit I wore every single day. There isn't a single event that jeans, Converse, t-shirt and biker jacket aren't suitable for and no one will ever convince me otherwise. I gave myself one last check in the mirror and poked aggressively at the lines that were rapidly setting in around my eyes. Too much time staring at a computer screen and not enough time having fun, I sighed. Maybe it really was time I started going out with Zoe again. We'd certainly had fun over the years, even if some of the people she worked with brought me out in hives.

I'd left it late before walking back into town for the gig and most of the audience had already gone in. I walked straight past the door security with nothing more than a nod—there's no need for guest passes when you're the default music columnist for the only local newspaper. They all knew who I was, even if I was more likely to be attending the Christmas panto than the re-emergence of a legendary rock band. Taking a deep breath, I headed into the auditorium. It was absolutely packed—clearly the city dwellers had made a rare trip out into the sticks. Most of the audience was male and middle-aged. Many of them were wearing ancient Black Swans tour t-shirts in order to set themselves apart from those who were just here out of curiosity and probably couldn't name three Black Swans singles if they tried. I could. I'd downloaded *See Me* the day after I'd first heard it played on a 'golden oldies' radio show—released before I was even born, it had been a slow-burner in the sort of grotty bars that Black Swans were still playing at the time, full of long-haired boys in ratty t-shirts and girls wearing flowery dresses with biker boots. *Long Goodbye* surprised everyone by hitting number one on the mainstream charts a year later, probably helped by the British music press being desperate to find some home-grown talent to balance the burgeoning American grunge scene that was sweeping everything before it in a tsunami of plaid shirts and scruffy hair. But my favourite Black Swans song was the one that turned out to be their last hit. *My Heart* finally sent them absolutely orbital—global number ones and a fanatical following across every continent—at the precise moment Marc Gatton crashed and burned. They were due to start a world tour the week after he'd nearly died in that Soho gutter and for a couple of days, the official line was that he had just been doing too much and everything would go ahead as planned. Just twenty-four hours before Black Swans were expected to fly out to Philadelphia for the first date of the tour, the entire lot was pulled. Apologies were made, refunds were issued and Marc Gatton was the talk of the music press—for about a week. And then someone even more famous than him went and died in even grubbier circumstances and Black Swans were consigned to the history books. Until now.

With a bit of determination, I managed to elbow my way through the crowd into position at the outer edge of the security barriers. Just as I forced my way past a balding, red-faced bloke dressed in a very whiffy 1992 tour t-shirt, the house lights dropped and the crowd roared. As I was jostled around by a group of excitable older women who were definitely going to feel it in the morning, there was movement in the darkness. The instrumental section of Black Swans—Paul Fisher on guitar, tall and dark and lithe as a big cat; the short and slightly balding Stef Matheson on drums and Kieran O'Reilly (Canadian, despite the name) on bass—walked out into the stage lights one at a time, grinning and nodding at the audience as they took their places. A blonde, boyish roadie held a small torch out in front of them, making sure no one fell flat on their faces before they even started. The band kicked into the first song and I could see Marc outlined against the backdrop, waiting for his moment. The roadie patted his arm in the gloom, as if attempting to calm his nerves. As the noise built, he stepped into the spotlight and the crowd surged forward, forcing me hard against the barriers. Just as I was about to turn and yell at whoever had just trodden hard on the back of my ankle, Marc strode over to our end of the barriers and I got my first real look at him. *Fucking hell.* I was pretty sure it was illegal to still be that handsome after so many years of hard living. The face that had stared out at me from so many magazines was now creased enough to prove that he hadn't been tempted down the cosmetic surgery route, but his jewel-green eyes were as sharp as they'd ever been. His dark hair was cut short, sticking out at angles that suggested he'd just got out of the shower, the stage lights picking out faint grey streaks at his temples. He was wearing a loose white shirt over

14

faded black jeans that were wedged into a pair of the pointiest snakeskin ankle boots I'd ever seen. Whatever he'd been doing during his years of exile had clearly paid off. Telling myself that I was noting these details for use in my review rather than my midnight fantasies—*yeah, right*—I studied him closely as he raced around the stage with the energy of a man half his age. He certainly still had it, whatever 'it' was. I let myself be swayed back and forth by the crowd, thoroughly enjoying the feeling of being this close to someone who a decade or so ago could have had my knickers on the floor with nothing more than a glance. In fact, maybe he still could. Unable to tear my eyes away, I wondered what it would be like to push my hands through that dark hair, to run my tongue down the side of his damp neck, to straddle him and—the overexcited man next to me chose that moment to throw both his arms up into the air, cheering loudly as he smacked me in the side of the face. He didn't even realise he'd knocked me, let alone ruined my fantasies. Marc was leaning against Paul now, the two men singing to each other with an intimacy that would have been impossible to fake and only escaped being embarrassing because they'd been doing it for decades. Then Marc broke his pose, strode across the front of the stage and was suddenly right in front of me. Even in the heaving crowd I jolted with the shock of his eyes boring into mine. He didn't so much as break a note, but the intensity with which he looked at me made me blush to my roots, my insides clenching with adrenalin. He reached across the barrier and I felt his slender fingers caressing the side of my face. Still singing, he trailed down my cheek and touched the edge of my lips, which parted without any conscious decision whatsoever. His thumb pressed against my teeth for the briefest of moments and I closed my eyes.

Then as quickly as he'd appeared in front of me he vanished, racing along the front row in a hunt for the next person to join him in a private moment. Embarrassed by my own reaction, I stood motionless for a moment, being pushed by the crowd and trying to ignore the sideways glances from the people around me. A woman a few feet further down the barrier nudged her boyfriend, cupping her hand to shout something into his ear. He looked over at me briefly before turning back to his girlfriend and saying something that made them both laugh, before they went back to concentrating on the stage. Mortified, I turned and fought my way out of the crowd before I even realised what I was doing. Hot, embarrassed tears pricked behind my eyes as I shoved my way to the bar, which was mercifully empty.

Fuck, fuck, fuck. I was a thirty-year-old professional, not a hormonal teen. What the hell was I doing letting myself get carried away like that? I ordered a double vodka and lime from the barman, not caring that they had no ice and that the lime came from a bottle of supermarket cordial. Downing it in one, I shoved the stupid plastic beaker back and demanded a second. When it arrived I made my way to the furthest, darkest corner I could find, in order to sulk in peace. I slid down the wall and sat on the grubby floor, my head swirling with the feelings that Marc's brief touch had unleashed. It wasn't as if I had no love life—after all, I lived with Dan. Admittedly, things had tailed off over the last year or so—we were always so tired, or busy, or he was out late and I was asleep by the time he came in. And he'd learned early on in our relationship that waking me up for a quickie was a shortcut to a knee in the groin, because there's nothing either sexy or romantic about being humped in the manner of an over-enthusiastic Labrador when you're half asleep. But however much I thought I'd happily given up on passion, evidently my hormones felt differently. I swallowed my drink like medicine, feeling the warmth circulating and taking the edge off my nerves. I glared towards the stage as the short set drew towards its end, watching Marc throw himself into the crowd like a homecoming hero. I should have known it was a bad idea to come. I'd just get the interview over with and go home. Hopefully I could get through it without my dreams being shattered any further. As the band left the stage to raucous cheers I grabbed my bag and stalked out of the hall. The sooner this was over, the better.

I skulked in the theatre's atrium until most of the audience had left. The security guard standing next to the staircase that led up to the dressing rooms and offices gave me another nod of recognition. Like I said—small town syndrome.

"You here to talk to the band, Jem?" I nodded. "They're in the big rooms on the top floor," he said, as I headed past him up the stairs. "You can't miss it." A gilt-framed mirror on the landing showed up a pink rash of anxiety down my neck and I cursed quietly for allowing myself to get so wound up. But before I could get too deep into examining my own dubious motives, I arrived at the top floor and came face to face with a pair of burly private security guards.

"Hi," I said to the nearest guard, "I'm from the Mercury?" He was the best part of seven feet tall and so muscular that his head seemed to join directly onto his shoulders. "I'm here for the interview." No-Neck looked me up and down and clearly decided that I wasn't a threat.

"They're only just back up here," he said. "You'll have to wait." Marvellous. I glared, but he just stared back at me with a bland expression on his face. Eventually I gave up and stalked over to the window at the end of the corridor. Pushing it open, I perched myself on the sill and breathed in the cold air. Maybe I could just say hello and then leave as quickly as possible. That way I could tell Arthur truthfully that I'd spoken to them. Then I'd just go home and make up some bullshit for the article. I couldn't *not* do it—Arthur had been thrilled to bag the only pre-tour interview with Black Swans. I suspected it had been purely because the band's management saw us as easy publicity before they had to face the snark of the national music press. No-Neck pushed the dressing room door open a fraction and muttered to someone inside, before calling down to me in a disinterested tone.

"They'll see you now," he said. They? That might be good. If I spoke to the entire band, I could pad it out and just do my best to pretend Marc wasn't there. The second guard—shorter in height than the first, but still giving off the air of someone who ate steroids for breakfast—beckoned me back down the corridor and swung the door open.

"She's come to check up on you. Be gentle," he announced, giving me a gentle push inside and immediately shutting the door behind me. The tiny, overcrowded room was silent for a brief moment—and then everyone carried on as if I didn't exist. There were far too many people in here for such an enclosed space—condensation was already streaming down the dark grey walls and the air actually *tasted* thick. Kieran was busily searching through a cool box filled with beer cans and Stef lay sprawled on a large sofa with a giggling girl on either side. Some of the band had aged better than others and Stef wasn't one of them. He gestured at to me to come closer as I took a couple of careful steps into the room.

"Why don't you come sit down, love?" he leered. "You can sit on me if you like." One of the girls thumped him in the chest.

"Hey, stop it!" she squealed, laughing. "You're with us, remember?" She stared at me as if I was something she'd scraped off her shoe.

"I can see you're all busy," I said. "Don't let me stop you." I stepped over two people on the floor, one of whom appeared to be asleep. The girl next to Stef was giggling and drunkenly applying lipstick to his face. She barely even noticed when I trod heavily on her foot as I made my way past. I managed to clamber over bodies until I reached the door I'd spied on the other side and, with a sigh of relief, let myself in to the next room. It was cooler in here and clearly laid out for a better class of customer—bottles of mineral water were crammed onto a sideboard next to an ice bucket and a low table in the middle of the room was laid with delicate sandwiches and tiny cakes. I leaned back against the door to take a deep breath. And then almost leapt out of my skin when a voice spoke from close by.

"Bit much for you is it?" Marc Gatton was sitting on the floor next to my feet. Barefoot and dressed in nothing more than jeans and a faded Black Sabbath t-shirt, he had a bottle of water wedged between his knees and a book in his lap. Before I could think up anything approaching a witty retort, the door was shoved open from behind—and I was toppled head first into the buffet table.

EXIT EVERYTHING

"Oh my god I am *so* sorry!" Paul Fisher stood frozen in the doorway, looking horrified as I stared up at him from the floor. Behind him, one of the girls on the sofa had seen what was going on and, cackling, nudged Stef to look. Behind them, the blonde roadie I'd spotted on the stage leaned silently against the wall, watching my mortification with the faintest of smiles on her face. I scrambled to my feet, picked up my bag and glared angrily at Paul and then down at Marc, who was still sitting watching me from the floor. He smiled slowly as I stared back exactly like a particularly gormless rabbit in headlights.

"You from the paper, love?" asked Paul, shutting the door behind him and breaking the spell. I nodded, relieved to no longer have an audience. On the other hand, I *had* just fallen flat on my face in front of the one person I'd have really liked to have impressed. Paul seemed oblivious to any uncomfortable atmosphere and just grinned happily at me, waving a bottle in my direction. "Want a beer?" I nodded. Anything to lighten the mood.

"Thanks." I took the cold bottle gratefully. Paul sank down on a sofa across from Marc and grinned at me.

"Hit us with it, then," he said. He looked genuinely keen, which was more than could be said of his friend. Marc looked me straight in the eye, an expression of mild amusement on his face.

"Look, you've already decided what you're going to write, so let's just get it over with." His voice was softer than I'd expected, the north London accent softened by years of living abroad. And now he was going to spoil everything by being mean. Aah well. If I was going to have my illusions shattered, it might as well be done in spectacular style.

"There's no need to be like that, Marc," said Paul, genuine concern on his face. "We need the publicity, whether you like it or not. Give us a break, eh?" He looked at Marc, who continued to look me straight in the eye. It was like being stalked by a very handsome snake. I held Marc's gaze, daring him to say anything else.

"Well," I muttered eventually, "it's nice to meet you, too." To my surprise, Marc laughed.

"Touché, I guess. Shall we start again? I'm Marc and this is Paul," a nod from the sofa, "and we are very pleased to meet you." A brief smile. God he was gorgeous. Maybe this wouldn't be so terrible after all. "We're not going to talk to you about Black Swans though." Okay, so it was suddenly terrible again.

"What the fuck?" My voice was sharp.

"Because it's boring," Marc replied. Paul was nodding in agreement—so much for thinking he was on my side. "And it's all been said before. So from now on we're going to let the music speak for us." I finally lost my temper.

"That is utterly fucking *ridiculous*," I snorted. "Did you get that out of the handbook? *Cheesy Pop Stars 101*?" Marc's face tightened briefly, then smoothed back out.

"Well if that's how you want to play it, you won't get an article, will you?" Marc tilted his head quizzically. "Who gives a shit what we think, anyway?"

"Actually, I do." I retorted loudly. "And so, I would imagine, will all those people who waited around for years for you to reappear from your period of drug-fuelled navel-gazing. But don't you worry about that—just carry on with your self-obsessed bloody wallowing. I'm sure you can live without a pathetic little review from a small-town newspaper."

"Hey, that's not what we meant," protested Paul, but Marc put a hand up to shush him.

"Let her think what she likes," he said. "I've had it with hacks who think I should jump on their say so—I've paid enough over the years for everything I've done, why should I care what some bloody *girl* thinks of me?"

"It's not just you though, is it?" Paul shot back, now having apparently forgotten that I was even in the room. "It's the rest of us who have to take it as well. The others might be doing it for the money, but I've stuck with this because we're *mates*. Don't fuck it up now, Marc." They sat glaring silently at each other. What a bloody ridiculous situation. I stood up, shoving my dictaphone back into my bag. Gathering my things, I stared down at the two of them bickering like schoolboys. Arthur owed me one for this.

"This is clearly pointless," I informed them, "so I'll leave you to your evening. Good luck with everything." They were both silent, Marc with his eyes narrowed at me and Paul just looking utterly fed up. I felt sorry for him—he seemed like a genuinely nice bloke and he'd somehow ended up with Prick of the Century for a best mate. "I mean it," I said. "Good luck. Because I think you're going to need it. Don't worry," this was to Paul, who was looking genuinely crestfallen, "it's not as if the opinion of a *girl* matters, is it? No one cares what I think." For the first time, a glimmer of embarrassment showed in Marc's eyes. In a fit of bravado, I grabbed an unopened bottle of Grey Goose that was sitting on a dressing table next to a generic welcome card from the theatre's management. "And I'll be taking this," I said, waving the bottle at them, "because I bloody well need it." With that, I stalked out of a door I'd spotted at the far end of the room. Thankfully, my panicked guess at the hotel's layout had been correct and the door took me back out onto the landing at the far end of the building. Way past the point of caring about minor things such as alarm systems, I pushed open the emergency door to the fire escape. There were no sudden sirens; I suspected that the management had switched it all off in the sure knowledge that a large group of drunken musicians were likely to be setting it off all night anyway. Closing the door carefully behind me, I went halfway down the first flight of stairs so that I couldn't be seen from the corridor, then slumped down on the metal step and leaned back against the cold brick wall. I was pretty sure this was the worst day of my working life. Not only had my dream man turned out to be a walking nightmare, I'd managed to look an idiot in front of him and his friends. *And don't forget the audience at the gig*, muttered a traitorous voice in the back of my head. I sighed, remembering the way Marc had touched me and how I'd reacted like a lovesick teenager. I just hoped it hadn't been witnessed by anyone who knew Dan. I was pretty sure he wouldn't take offence—he was confident enough in my loyalty that it wouldn't occur to him that I might ever be tempted—but he'd find it ridiculously funny. Probably to the point of making me the butt of puerile jokes for the next six months. It would be a long time before I'd be able to face going to the pub with him and his friends.

The least Marc Gatton owed me was a free drink. Unscrewing the cap of the vodka, I took a deep gulp and spluttered as it hit my throat. Not for the first time that night, I wished I hadn't given up smoking as a thirtieth birthday present to myself. I could see a coach with blacked out windows tucked away at the far corner of the car park. Hopefully it was the band's tour bus—I'd just have to wait until they'd left, then sneak out from the back of the building. The sooner I was home in bed and this stupid day was over, the better. I jumped as my phone pinged loudly in my pocket. It was a text from Tris.

'Have you had your wicked way with him yet then?' followed by an obscene amount of sticky-out tongue emojis. I smiled at his predictability.

'Not in a million bloody years. Will give you gory details tomorrow.' A response pinged back immediately.

'You'd better! By the way, Simon is DELICIOUS!' Just then, the fire door opened with a clunk behind me. Whipping round, I saw an outline in the shadows above me and realised with a sinking heart that it was Marc. And he was staring straight at me.

'I hope you're enjoying our booze,' he said lightly. I dropped the phone into my bag and glared silently up at him. He stepped out onto the metal platform of the fire escape. 'Was I really that awful to talk to?' His voice was soft and quiet.

"Actually yes," I said, the combination of vodka and frustration making me braver than usual. "Yes, you were." I stood up, the bottle still in my hand. "I was just trying to do my job—my stupid, *suburban* job—" he winced at that, "and you were, indeed, bloody rude." He leant back against the doorframe, looking strangely young and vulnerable in the subdued light from the corridor.

"Perhaps we could start again," he offered. I glared at him.

"I'm not sure I want to bother," I retorted. "I've seen enough to give me plenty to write about."

"You didn't fancy joining the party, then?" I shook my head and he laughed ruefully. "I'm clean these days," he said, raising his water bottle up in salute, "which is more than I can say for the others. The only other one that seems to have grown up any is Paul. So I find it easier to stay out of the way and avoid speaking to people. Avoiding temptation." A sideways look. "Apart from when temptation comes and sits down in my quiet space, of course." I felt myself blush in the darkness, embarrassment making my words sharper than I intended.

"Do you often grope random audience members?" Tipping the bottle back, I took another drink. Wiping my mouth, I looked him straight in the eye. Dark eyes locked on mine and for a second I felt the world shift on its axis. Oh shit. But I didn't move an inch, held by a tight fascination that was making my stomach curl and the hair stand up on the back of my neck.

"I don't make a habit of it, no." He took a step down towards me. I knew it was probably a bad idea to let him continue, but when was I ever going to get this opportunity again? My teenage self would stab me in the eye if I walked out now. Distracted, I let go of the heavy vodka bottle and it bounced, falling onto to the street below. The noise of it smashing into tiny pieces across the pavement broke the tense atmosphere. "Wait right there," he said suddenly, "I've got an idea." He disappeared back into the corridor, closing the door firmly behind him. I was alone outside on a fire escape again and I didn't even have the vodka as a consolation prize. Marvellous. *Excellent* day's work there, Jemimah. But before I could think about just making a run for it, a light came on in a window on the floor below me. A moment later it opened and Marc poked his head out, twisting round to peer up to where I perched on the fire escape. "Come on," he said, "it's warmer in here." I walked down slowly, wondering how on earth I was supposed to get inside. There was no door at this level. "Through the window," said Marc, answering my question. Shaking my head at the absurdity of the situation, I threw my bag into the room ahead of me and then pulled myself up onto the windowsill. I tried to swing my legs around as elegantly as possible in the cramped space, but caught my foot on the frame and would have toppled headfirst had Marc not grabbed me. We locked eyes and it might have turned out like one of the trashy romances that Tris loved to read behind the reception desk, if I hadn't somehow managed to hang onto my last shreds of self-respect. I pulled away, making an unnecessary show of dusting myself down. Marc gave a small smile and turned to a mini-bar cabinet in the corner of the room. "If I know our manager," he said, pulling cupboard doors open, "he'll have made sure he was well supplied—ha!" He turned back to me, with a fresh bottle in his hand. "Hope you like gin?" I nodded. "And there's ice and tonic," he grinned, "so we can be more civilised."

I checked out my surroundings whilst the most unlikely barman I'd ever met poured me a drink. He stuck with his bottle of water, but poured the contents into a glass and added ice and lemon. We were in one of the fancy meeting rooms that the theatre hired out to companies who wanted to appear wealthier than they really were. I knew from friends who'd worked there that renting out the rooms made the theatre more money than its actual events and strongly suspected that it would eventually find itself converted into yet another soulless hotel. The room was lit only by a couple of expensive-looking table lamps and was surprisingly cosy. Marc followed my gaze and grinned. Close up, he was like a handsome, overgrown kid; clear-eyed and excitable.

"Mike was using it earlier," he said. "I took the keys from him and said I needed to do a last minute interview."

I raised my eyebrows. "Is this how you always conduct interviews?"

He looked sheepish. "I'm really sorry about earlier," he said, "honestly I am. But I'm not very good with people. Here—" he handed me a heavy glass that contained what smelled like the strongest G&T ever, "especially when I fancy them." He stopped speaking and looked so stricken that I almost laughed out loud. "Oh god, I'm sorry. Again. That sounded really clichéd, didn't it?"

"It did," I agreed, but in my head an excitable voice was screeching *oh my god oh my god oh my god* because somehow I was alone with Marc Gatton, drinking a G&T that he'd poured for me and he'd openly declared his interest. This was *not* how I'd expected my evening to pan out, not even in my wildest fantasy. The best I'd hoped for was a quick chat, for us to not hate each other and maybe a promise to keep vaguely in touch. That way I'd have been able to claim him as a friend and thus gained myself some cool points with Tris and Zoe, without having done anything too dramatic and applecart-upsetting. But right now, it felt distinctly as though the entire room was filled with applecarts and they were all more than ready to topple. "So, what's the story with the false snark?" I asked, reluctantly forcing myself back to the day job. Marc sat down on a large squishy sofa and gestured for me to join him. I did so, but purposely sat as far away as possible and turned to face him, pulling my knees up as an extra barrier. I also pulled my voice recorder out of my bag, balancing it on my knees. Marc gazed at it.

"Can't we just chat," he asked, "without that thing being on?" He nodded at the recorder.

"Can you try not being a grade-A prick?" He raised an eyebrow, and then laughed.

"I wish more journalists were like you," he said. "Does your boss mind you being this rude to people?" I shrugged.

"I'm pretty sure that my boss would understand, considering how I've been treated so far. Look," I took a deep breath and decided to go with the truth, "I've been a fan for years and couldn't pass up the opportunity to come meet you all in person."

"And then I ruined it by being a grade-A prick," observed Marc, drily.

"Nah," I said, "you'd already made me feel like a first class idiot by poking my teeth at the gig," I sighed. "What was that even *about*, for fucks sake?" Marc was silent for a moment.

"I don't know," he finally said, "and that's the honest answer. I just saw you and it happened before I'd even really thought about it. It's certainly not something I make a habit of." He looked thoughtful. "Actually, it's the only time I've ever done it. And I really don't know why. Does that make me a terrible person?" I considered this and then sat up, slipping the voice recorder back into my bag.

"No, I don't think you're a terrible person," I said. "But I could do with another drink." Marc grinned and got up, taking my glass from me and heading over to the mini-bar. I stood up and walked over to the window for the sake of something to do.

"I like looking out at the night," said Marc softly, making me jump for the second time that evening.

"Stop creeping up on me!" I squeaked, turning to glare at him. And then, before I'd even registered what I was doing, I was kissing him hard, full on the mouth. He tensed for a fraction of a second, then grabbed my head in both hands and kissed me back with flattering ferocity. I let myself enjoy it for a few seconds before pulling away, leaving him looking decidedly off-balance. "Now you know how it feels to be grabbed without warning," I said, rescuing my glass from his hand and raising it. "Cheers." He looked utterly dumbstruck for a second and then grabbed me. The glass finally went flying as I slid my hands up underneath his t-shirt, my nails scraping hard across his back. He had my hair clenched in one hand whilst the other slid up my tshirt, squeezing my breasts before reaching round to unclasp my bra.

"Nifty move," I allowed, pulling away from him slightly. He pulled my t-shirt up and over my head and swung my bra from the end of his long, slim fingers like a very masculine burlesque dancer.

"Misspent youth," he grinned, before leaning in to kiss me some more. We fell onto the sofa together like hormonal teenagers at their first co-ed party. I kicked my boots off and they went flying across the room, hitting an expensive-looking sideboard with a heavy thump. Marc kept kissing me, running his tongue along the edge of my teeth and only breaking away briefly, to allow me to drag his t-shirt off over his head. I pushed blindly at the waistband of his jeans, desperate now.

"Shall I just take them off?" Before I could answer, he stood up and slid out of them in one fluid movement, straightening up in front of me absolutely naked but for the tattoos that I recognised from so many promo photos. His battered body had worn better than it deserved to, after such excess—tight and hard, stomach muscles clearly outlined in the shadows. I trailed my fingers along the fine line of dark hair that headed down from his waist and he sucked a breath. "Excuse me for sounding like a teenager," his voice sounded loud in the empty room, "but I don't suppose you carry condoms on a work trip?" I was stunned for a second, and then laughed.

"You're in luck," I said. "There might be one in my bag. Assuming it hasn't outlived its expiry date." *Thank you Zoe, I* thought, *thank you for your years of usually pointless yet endlessly hopeful prepping.* I looked him in the eye, so close that I could feel his breath on my face. "Surely you ought to be more prepared yourself, if you make a habit of this sort of thing?" Marc grinned.

"I'd be embarrassed to admit just how little I do this sort of thing," he confessed. "Anyway," he said, sliding a confident hand down between my legs and making me squeak, "you were saying you'd check your bag?" I leant over and grabbed my satchel from the floor, scrabbling around amongst the detritus at the bottom until I found the little foil packet. Marc held out his hand and I passed it over, telling myself that this was a perfectly normal situation, that of course I was alone half naked with my all time heart throb who was right this minute—*oh dear gods this was really happening*—expertly rolling a condom down his impressive erection. I couldn't take my eyes off him. He gazed back calmly.

"Now, I think it's your turn to get naked, don't you?" With that he gave me a sharp push backwards onto the sofa and was eagerly tugging my jeans down my wriggling legs when there was a knock at the door. "Shit," he muttered. "Who is it?" his voice was sharp in the quiet room. I lay staring at the ceiling, trying not to think about how I was naked on a sofa with Marc Gatton looming above me and how I would not be responsible for my actions if we were disturbed now.

"It's Paul," came a muffled voice through the door. "Bus is leaving soon, you'd better shift your arse if you want to get back into town tonight." Marc cursed under his breath. I could hear the drunken party from upstairs grumbling and cackling their way along corridors and down the stairs.

"You go on without me," he said at the closed door, looking down at me with a grin. "I'm just reading and catching up with some emails, I'll get a cab later." He leant forward and finished pulling my jeans off, and then slid a hand up my leg and under my knicker elastic. I shut my mouth tight in an attempt to stay silent as he wriggled my underwear off and pinged the scrap of fabric across the room.

"Can't you do all that back at the hotel?" Paul's voice sounded uncertain. "Mike won't like it."

"Mike can fuck off," Marc said loudly. "It's about time he remembered that he's our manager, not our owner." Paul snorted.

"Try telling that to his missus," he said. "She'll be wanting to show you off to her friends back at the hotel. Like a pet monkey."

"All the more reason for me not to go," replied Marc, flatly. I closed my eyes and tried to work out how the hell I'd got into this situation. "Anyway I'll be there at some point," he carried on. "The night is yet young, as they say." I opened my eyes to a wicked grin that made me blush to my roots. "Piss off, mate," he said to the closed door, "I'll text you in a bit."

"Charming," came Paul's muffled response. Neither of us moved as we listened to him leave. It wasn't until there was silence outside that I dared breathe properly again. Marc was grinning down at me and—impressively, given the circumstances—clearly hadn't lost physical interest.

"Where were we?" He knelt down and I wrapped my legs around him as if it was the most natural thing in the world, pulling him down and gasping as he slid inside. *God*, he felt good. It was a long, long time since sex with Dan had been anything but perfunctory. I still wasn't convinced that this was the right thing to do, but there couldn't be many more acceptable reasons than the chance to shag someone you'd fancied from afar for years, could there? I'd worry about motives in the morning, when Marc was long gone and I could chalk it up to experience. In the meantime, right here and right now I was naked in a hotel room with Marc bloody Gatton and he was moving in ways that were making me squeak and oh my god I could never tell anyone about this because they wouldn't believe me but Jesus it felt good and I needed him to not stop, not ever... He leant down and kissed me without breaking rhythm and I pulled him even tighter against me, not wanting to let him go.

Afterwards we clung to each other, both panting slightly as we stared up at the ceiling. This certainly wasn't the end to the evening that I'd imagined when I'd walked out of the Black Swans gig only a couple of hours earlier. I suddenly felt rather awkward and possibly in need of making a fast escape, but Marc didn't seem to agree. He sat up and reached for a throw

morning, apparently. Well I guess time flew when you were having fun. I snorted quietly to myself, and then froze as Marc stirred.

"You okay? I'm not squashing you?" His voice was soft and sleepy and he dozed back off before I could respond. I must have fallen asleep as well, because the next time I opened my eyes it was almost light. Marc was still flat out, one hand clamped firmly across my chest. He looked so much younger like this, his face peaceful and a slight smile on his lips. He also had a noticeable erection, which I resisted the urge to wriggle against. I wondered what he was dreaming about. I found myself inspecting him closely, trying to make some sense of him lying asleep next to me as if it was the most natural thing in the world. This couldn't be real. The more I thought about it, the more convinced I became that I should just leave, before Marc woke up and the cold light of reality broke the spell. At least that way no one would know what had happened and I could—hopefully—salvage some professional integrity. I didn't make a habit of sleeping with my interviewees. But then my interviewees were usually champion potato growers or dog breeders in their eighties who'd have a heart attack at the mere thought. I slid out from under Marc's arm and managed to clamber over the back of the sofa, only just avoiding landing face first on the carpet. I'd make a useless cat burglar. Creeping round the room I found my jeans, bra and t-shirt, but not my knickers. Fuck it; he could keep them as a souvenir. I pulled my clothes on as quickly as I could, but couldn't find my boots. After a minor panic at the thought of having to walk barefoot through Uppingwood town centre, I spotted them flung into a corner on the opposite side of the room. As I pulled them on, I grinned at the recollection of just how quickly we'd got undressed. Picking up my bag, I snuck out of the room as quietly as possible, stopping for one last glance back at Marc, still snoring gently on the sofa. Last night had undeniably been one of my more memorable assignments, but there was no way I was going to hang around until he woke up and we both had to endure the embarrassment of him trying to remember my name. I made my way back out to the main corridor, stepping carefully over the empty bottles and spilled food that trailed out of the Black Swans' rooms and all the way down the stairs. I didn't envy the staff finding this mess when they got into work—although they might have an interesting surprise when they went into the furthest conference room. I felt a twinge of guilt at not waking Marc, but dismissed it. He was a big boy—*literally*, I sniggered to myself—and he could look after himself. Skipping down the stairs with an energy that I was fairly confident wasn't going to last, I saw that a pair of cleaners had just starting work in the atrium. Doing my best to act as though it was entirely normal for a disheveled woman to appear out of nowhere in a supposedly empty theatre, I smiled broadly, nodded a brief good morning at them and sailed out through the front doors, leaving them staring after me in confusion.

GUILTY SECRETS

Catching a glimpse of my reflection in a shop window, I realised that emergency repairs were needed if I was going to go straight into work. Which was clearly my only option at this time in the morning, because otherwise I risked having to talk to Dan. Oh god, *Dan*. Fuck. What on earth was I doing? I had a perfectly nice life and a decent boyfriend. Okay, sometimes I'd like a bit more excitement in my life. But Dan was loyal, which was more than I could say for myself right now. He hadn't even texted to ask why I hadn't come home—he must have just assumed I'd met up with Zoe. It was probably better not to disturb him anyway, I decided. I'd head into work and get my shit together before talking to anyone. I strode down the high street, trying my best to give off an air of merely having a busy start to my morning. The newsagent on the corner was open and, as if by some beautiful gift from the heavens, had toothbrushes on the shelves next to the painkillers. Brush, paste, baby wipes—an emergency wash kit would have to do. Grabbing a large bar of chocolate and a can of Coke that wasn't as cold as I'd have liked, I checked my phone whilst a sullen young man behind the till rang up my bill. I'd never been in the shop this early in the day before and was quite relieved to be served in silence rather than by the jolly and talkative Polish woman who was usually there. It was a bright sunny morning as I headed down towards the Mercury building with a grin plastered across my face. I wondered whether Marc had woken up yet. Would he be disappointed when he realised I'd gone? I went over the night's activities in my head in order to burn them into my memories. I'd forgotten just how lovely it was to be with someone who seemed genuinely interested in me. And Marc was…well; Marc Gatton was a much nicer person that I'd thought he was going to be. Sweet, almost. Yup—even if I never saw him again, it would be a good memory.

I was still smiling as I got into the office, relieved that I'd have an hour to sort myself out before anyone else arrived. Brushing my teeth over the sink in the ladies' loo made me feel more human. I cleaned my face with the baby wipes and, by the time I'd done some basic repair work with the bits of old makeup scattered in my bag, I felt I was marginally less likely to terrify people with my deathly appearance. After punching at the coffee machine until it begrudgingly delivered a large black Americano, I flung myself down at my desk to finally check through my phone messages. The first was from Tris.

'I have just had THE *filthiest sex, you would not believe it - tell you all soonest!*' I really hoped he wouldn't. Tris had an unfortunate habit of treating me to more detail than a good friend deserved. On the other hand, maybe he'd be so distracted by his latest conquest that he wouldn't question me too much about my own evening. Then three from Zoe.

'*Are you at the gig? Have you managed to speak to Gatton without tripping over your own tongue? Tell me all!*'

'*FFS, I need updates, woman! You'd better have no phone signal or at least be dead. Ring me first thing.'*

'If you don't call me I will call you around lunchtime. Am heading to yet ANOTHER shop opening, borrrrrrring. Save me with gossip!'

The last one had arrived only five minutes earlier; I must have missed the bleep whilst cleaning my teeth. She wouldn't be palmed off, I knew that much. I'd have to give her a sort-of version of last night, without mentioning the interview-that-wasn't. And the copious amounts of gin, and the rampant sex and…oh bloody hell, I really had spent the night with the one person I never thought I'd even *meet*, let alone have a midnight heart-to-heart with. And the sex, *oh* the sex…I spun around on my chair, snorting with glee. And I'd left him there to wake up alone. In the cold light of day I couldn't decide if that had been the best, or—quite possibly—the worst decision of my life. Oh well, it was too late to worry about it now. I shuffled some papers out onto my desk so that it would at least look as if I was working, drained the rest of my coffee then lay my head on my hands. A quick doze would help, before the others came in.

'Good morrrrrrrning, Jemimah!' *Shit.* Tris's dulcet tones about three inches from my left ear gave me such a fright that I shot upright at high speed and nearly fell off my chair. I blinked and tried to focus as he perched himself on my desk and sat waiting expectantly, with his arms folded and eyebrows raised. "Had a good night, did we?" he asked, archly. "Still wearing last night's clothes, are we?" He actually sniggered. I glared back at him.

"Different jeans," I muttered unconvincingly. Tris snorted. "Anyway, what happened with you?" Attack was always the best form of defence. "Pleasant evening with Simon, was it?"

He bit. Thank fuck for gossipy boys.

"Oh my god it was *amazing*. Honestly Jem, I think this might be *it*." He swung himself dramatically around and off the desk. "He is *perfect*. Sweet and funny and has the tightest buttocks you have ever seen on a man." He made hand gestures to illustrate the perfection of said buttocks. "Can I just tell you—"?

"No!" I interrupted. "No you cannot tell me, because I don't want to know. Whatever it might be." I ignored his hurt expression. "I have to see Simon over the coffee machine, I don't want to know *anything* about his buttocks, thank you very much. Now go sit at your desk and look pretty, there's a good boy."

"You are a heartless wretch, Jemimah Holliday." Tris stuck his tongue out at me, and then swanned off down to reception, whistling as he went. The rest of the morning was easy. Arthur didn't get in until ten and barely spoke. A brief, "Hope it went well, get it done by end of day" and he was safely shut in his office. I heard the racing commentary start and knew I wouldn't be bothered for another couple of hours. But I did have to write the Black Swans piece—and I wasn't sure how I was going to manage it. Copious amounts of outright lying and blushing to the roots of my hair, probably. I hadn't taken a single note, either at the gig or afterwards, although I was pretty sure that *'Gatton has a strong presence on stage and even more so in the sack'* would be enough to send Mercury readers into a vapour. I took the sensible and obvious course of ignoring it entirely, in favour of finishing a report on the merger of two local toddler groups. My phone rang dead on midday.

"Hey, super girl," said Zoe, struggling to be heard over the noise in the background. "I'm still stuck at this opening. Currently pretending to eat canapés with reality TV stars who don't know a midi hem from their own arse, but no change there." I grinned. "So, how was last night? Tell me *all* about it!"

"There isn't much to tell," I fibbed. "The gig was great," that was true enough, "and Marc's looking really well. Didn't have much to say though." I wasn't *exactly* lying—the only conversation we'd had was definitely destined for the confidential files.

"Ugh, what a disappointment," sighed Zoe. Christ, if only she knew. "Anyway just make it up from the press releases, blah blah. He's on television tonight, apparently. I might record it, just to see what he looks like these days."

"That's the first I've heard of it," I said, nervously swinging around on my chair, "what's he on?" I wondered if I could bear to watch him at such a distance, considering how close we'd been the night before. I wriggled in my seat at the recollection.

"It's the Saturn Awards—they're the not-actually-a-surprise-at-all surprise guests. Lifetime achievement award, or something. Not sure how they've got that, considering they haven't been around for years. Friends in the right places, I guess." Zoe sniffed. "Anyway I'm not supposed to know and neither are you. Although we've had a press release to the office about it, so it's not much of a secret." I perched on my chair, hugging my knees.

"Well I might watch then," I said, "if I'm not busy." Who was I kidding? I'd be there in front of the screen for the duration, like some lovesick fan.

"Probably best to not bother, if he's that much of a disappointment." Zoe sounded almost pleased. "Anyway I need to go look interested in very uninteresting people. Catch up soon? Drag yourself into town and we'll go drink too much gin in whichever bar Cynthia deems the hippest this week." Cynthia was entertainments editor at the Gossip—all sharp hair and even sharper sniping skills. I'd never been keen on her, but Zoe liked the VIP invites that came with being Cynthia's office buddy.

"Yeah, okay," I tried to sound enthusiastic. "Sounds good."

"Force yourself to have fun, Jem," Zoe laughed, "you might find you enjoy it. Anyway, good luck with the article and whatever else you're doing in Snoozeville—I'll call you in the week." And with that, she rang off.

THROUGH THE LOOKING GLASS

"Hey, sleepyhead," Tristan's voice cut across the quiet room. I was the only person who bothered to look up. It was mid-afternoon and the entire office was trying not to fall asleep, all hoping that no one else would notice. Tris was heading towards me with a shit-eating grin on his face and the biggest bouquet of flowers I'd ever seen in my life cradled in his arms. "These are apparently for you. At least," he peered at the card on the wrap, "that is, if you can be described as '*Beautiful Jemimah*', given the state you're currently in. And oh," he flicked the card off the plastic and held it aloft in order to read the handwritten message better, "they are from 'M'. Now who could M be, we are all wondering? Hmmm?" I held my hands out for the flowers and Tris spiked the card into the top before handing them over. The huge fountain of dark green foliage with purple and black blooms was tied with heavy cerise ribbon and I very much doubted it had come from the florist down the road, which was more your 'traditional weddings and funerals' type. I looked at the card.

Beautiful Jemimah. Green for your eyes, black for my heart. Car will collect you at 5pm, if you can bear to see me again. There'll be time to change out of last night's clothes when you get to the hotel—I'll arrange it all. Let's have some fun. M x

I felt a wave of sudden panic rising in my throat. I hadn't actually considered the possibility of seeing him again. Or that he'd even *want* to, for that matter. There was no way I could meet him tonight, not at a big event. I wouldn't know how to handle it. What if I made myself look like even more of an idiot than I'd managed already? On the other hand, Zoe would never forgive me if I turned down such an invite, with its promise of gossip and glamour (although she might also never forgive me for going without her). Perhaps I could convince myself it was just a normal job and fake being a grown up. I'd had to do press screenings in the past—surely an awards ceremony was much the same, just with added glitz? I was definitely not feeling much like a professional adult right now though, that was certain. And I looked like *shit*. I wouldn't be able to go home first, either. I could probably get away with messaging Dan to say I had work on, but I wasn't sure whether I was capable of lying directly to his face. Fuck, fuck, *fuck*. I pushed the flowers back at Tris, who looked surprised.

"Can you stick them in water for me?" I asked him. "I need to go out." His eyebrows shot up. "I'll explain later—I need a new outfit. *Work*," I snapped at his open-mouthed gaping. "Bloody Marc Gatton," I grumbled, as I rooted around under the desk for my bag, "I can't believe I'm having to do this."

"Do what?" asked Tris. "Sell your body? Your *soul?*"

"I hope not," I muttered as I grabbed my wallet and shot out of the door. Uppingwood wasn't exactly a hotbed of fashion stores, but maybe I could get something just a bit less skanky than last night's jeans. "I *really* hope not."

46

us," she said in a delighted tone, heading over to me. "I'll take her," she said to the porter. With that, she picked up my bags in one hand and linked the other through my arm, scooping me up and heading back towards the lifts.

"I'm Suzie," she said. "Paul's wife. I'm under strict instructions to look after you."

"Paul? Isn't Marc here? I had a message from him earlier. I think." I trailed off.

"You'll have to forgive the boys today," Suzie said with a rueful smile. "Big night tonight and they're all super nervous. It'll be fine though," she dropped my arm to press the call button on the lift, "it always is. Got nine lives, has our Marc." The doors pinged open. She stepped inside and I followed her like a child. She seemed friendly enough, so I decided to be honest.

"I have absolutely no idea what is going on," I confessed.

Suzie laughed. "You," she poked me in the ribs, "are coming out with us tonight. Well, with me, actually." She hoisted my bag onto her shoulder. "Marc asked me to babysit you. Or rather, he said I was to keep an eye on you so that you didn't run away." She pressed the button for the top floor and peered at me through long lashes as we swept silently upwards. "He likes you. He says you're different. Well all hail that, I say." She grinned. The lift doors opened onto a plush corridor. "We're in the penthouse," she said. "Mind you, it's only because the organisers are paying for it—Mike would have them in a hostel if it meant more money for him."

"Their manager?"

"Yup." Suzie pulled a face. "I've never liked him, but he's been with the band from the start and they're a loyal bunch. Must be, to have come back after Marc's issues." I felt slightly uncomfortable.

"You do know I'm writing about them?" I asked finally. "I'm supposed to be doing a piece on Black Swans. Only for a local paper though, nothing dreadful." We'd come to a halt outside a large, heavy-looking door and Suzie turned to look at me as she fished in her handbag for the entry card. "Oh but this isn't work," she said happily, as the door swung open. "This is pleasure." She grinned at me. "Let's have some fun."

The room was huge. Correction—rooms. Plural. The suite contained a living room and enormous bathroom, plus what looked suspiciously like a large double bedroom at the back. To my surprise, Suzie handed me the door card.

"This is yours," she said. "Marc thought you'd like the space to get ready. Me and Paul are in the next suite down—we got number one because it's bigger. You'll recognise it by the sound of the screeching kids. I brought them with me," she explained, "along with my mother, god bless her saintly soul. They'll do more for Nana than they'll do for me, I can tell you that for nothing." She dropped down onto the nearest sofa. "So," she said appraisingly, "what are you going to wear? I've been told to take you shopping." I felt a flush rising on my neck. I opened my bag to pull out the dress I'd bought earlier.

"This. I'm wearing this," I said firmly, giving the dress a shake in Suzie's direction, "and I'm not going to be bought by some ageing rock star, thank you very much."

Suzie laughed. "Good for you," she cackled. "I'm not surprised Marc likes you. Not enough people stand up to him, in my opinion. It's a novelty for all of us." She stood up. "There's a few things you might need in the bathroom, anyway—I just bought one of everything. He wasn't sure you'd have had time to go home, apparently. Sounds like you kids had a good time last night." She grinned and my stomach lurched. "Marc tells me the pair of you sat and chatted for ages," she continued and I started breathing again. "He certainly seems to have enjoyed himself. Sometimes, talking's the most intimate thing you can do with another person, don't you think?" I just stared silently at her in response. "Shout if you need anything," she continued, as she headed back out into the corridor, "I need to go see the brats before bedtime. You get yourself ready and I'll be back at seven thirty—we'll head down to the show together."

"I, err, okay," I floundered as she headed to the door. "And thank you."

"No problem," she grinned, and the door closed with a thump.

I decide to explore my surroundings. All hotel rooms were pretty much the same when it came down to it—this one was just bigger than most and had better quality toiletries in the bathroom. A large wicker basket next to the sink appeared to contain one of everything you might find in the women's section of a pharmacy, with some extras just in case. Not only had Suzie thought to include razors and a toothbrush, there was mascara, concealer that by some miracle was the correct shade, a selection of lipsticks—it was a good job I liked red—and a variety of hair styling products. She'd even added tampons, moisturiser and perfume. I checked my phone whilst running a bath and tried not to be disappointed that there wasn't anything from Marc. There was, however, a message from Dan.

'Dirty stop out! Say hi to Zoe for me. Let me know what time

you'll be in tonight and I'll cook.' Guilt gnawed at the pit of my stomach as I replied.

'Zoe says hi. I'm going to be out tonight as well—it's work stuff, will explain tomorrow. Really sorry.' Dan rarely actually spoke to Zoe. They pretended to be friends, but in reality they each saw the other as an alien species. Dan thought Zoe was shallow and silly, Zoe considered Dan boring and staid. And never the twain shall meet. Which worked very much in my favour right now, I thought to myself. A text from Zoe popped up. Speak of the devil, as my dad liked to say.

'Work gossip has it that Black Swans are definitely on tonight—don't forget to watch. Try not to lick the screen! Zx'

I'd rather be licking the real thing, I thought to myself. Maybe I would, later. I slid into the enormous, claw-footed bath and ducked my head under the bubbles in an attempt to drown the rising guilt. I was heading for crashing disappointment, I was sure of it. People like me didn't get to date rock stars. And I already had a boyfriend—I definitely needed to decide what to do about that at some point. But right now wasn't the time for introspection, what with being in a hotel room paid for by a rock star and lying in a bath getting ready to go out to see said rock star and, with any luck, finishing off the evening by riding the aforementioned rock star like a bony pony. I washed my hair in the bathwater as a dirty protest against my disconcertingly luxurious surroundings, then clambered out and wrapped myself in the biggest, fluffiest towel I'd ever seen. I caught sight of my own reflection in the huge bathroom mirror. My eyes glittered with excitement and I looked as though I was on heat. Christ, I'd need to put some of Suzie's concealer on my cheeks or I'd spend the evening looking as though I was having a hot flush. I was pretty sure that rock star companions didn't have hot flushes, not even the menopausal ones. Maybe they botox'd it into oblivion. The hotel hairdryer turned out to be far more powerful than my small one at home and I spent a good ten minutes detangling myself in order to avoid the 'dragged through a hedge backwards' look. Then I decided that it was actually quite a *good* look, and re-tangled it with the help of random bottles of styling spray that I unearthed from the basket. Resisting the urge to tip all the freebies into my bag like the ultimate suburban asshole, I got dressed and looked at myself in the long mirror. Not bad, actually. So long as I put plenty of eyeliner on and mussed my hair up a bit more it might pass as an intentional look, rather than a cosplay outfit based on the theme of 'spent the night drinking and having sex, before going straight to work without any sleep.' I dug out my makeup bag and did the best I could with a combination of its contents and Suzie's additions, then squirted an experimental cloud of perfume into the air from the bottle in the gift basket. I'd never heard of it but it smelled expensive, so I gave myself a good coating. According to my watch it was still only 7pm. I forced myself to sit down on the bed and switched on the television. As I flicked through the programmes, I stumbled on a music channel that was covering the awards ceremony. Two minutes later I was pacing the carpet and trying not to hyperventilate, after Marc had popped up on the television screen. I'd immediately switched it off in a blind panic, but not before registering that he'd clearly slept okay and also found time to have a shower and get changed. He was wearing a black silk shirt with black jeans over the top of pointed black Chelsea boots and looked for all the world like Lucifer on the sexiest day of his afterlife. *Aaargh.* What the fuck was I doing? Just as I was starting to hyperventilate, there was a loud banging on the door.

"Let me in!" yelled a muffled voice. Suzie. I pulled the door open so quickly she nearly fell inside. Regaining her balance she appraised me coolly. "You'll do," she decided. I took a deep breath in the hope of slowing my heart rate down to manageable levels.

"Well, thanks," I muttered eventually.

She laughed. "Marc was hoping to come fetch you," she said, "but an interview's run over time. I told Paul we'll just go down together and see them later." I wondered briefly if Marc's interviews were always as interesting as the one with me had been and tried not to feel sick. "Ready to go?"

"Ready as I'll ever be," I said, sounding utterly unconvincing. Suzie laughed and thumped my arm in what I assumed was supposed to be a supportive gesture.

"It'll be fine," she assured me. "You'll get used to this sort of thing soon enough." Grabbing my new clutch from the bed I shoved my phone and lipstick inside and decided it would have to do, only just remembering to pull the price tag off the bag's zipper. We headed out of the suite, Suzie leading me towards a different lift at the opposite end of the corridor. "You came in through the back entrance," she explained, "like a secret delivery." She cackled with laughter again. It was like being with a small, blonde witch. A pretty and very kind witch. She pressed the button and the doors pinged open. "This time we go public."

A (VERY PUBLIC) DEBUT

The lift doors opened onto absolute bedlam. Hundreds of people milled around in various groups, drinking and chatting. To my utter horror, there also appeared to be several film crews. Okay, so they were from music channels rather than the main networks, but the thought of potentially being caught on camera hadn't even occurred to me. How fucking naive was that? I suddenly felt queasy. Suzie caught hold of a passing waiter and grabbed two glasses of champagne.

"Take this," she said as she thrust a glass into my hand. "You'll need it." I watched her drain her glass in one go and neatly switch it for another full one off a passing tray.

"You make it sound like torture," I laughed nervously, struggling to be heard over the noise.

Suzie pulled a face. "When you look in on this life," she said. "It looks like Wonderland. Pose and smile!" I followed instructions and a flash blinded me. The cameraman walked off to find more victims as Suzie continued. "But it's nothing of the kind. The money and other luxuries are brilliant, obviously. But it's hard work and it can be miserable at times. Mostly," she grabbed two more glasses as another tray went by, "it's just fucking tedious. It's no wonder we all drink."

"Hey!" A tall woman in a gold lamé pantsuit was waving frantically at us as she headed determinedly towards us across the room. She had short, black pixie-cut hair and had enormous gold hoops hanging from her ears. Suzie's face lit up.

"Anna! Paul's first wife", she explained. I tried not to look too surprised as the women hugged. Suzie turned to me. "Anna, this is Jem," I moved to shake her hand, but she hugged me as well, before stepping back and grinning, still holding my arms. "Jem is going to give our Marc his chance to finally play nice," Suzie said. "Aren't you, Jem?"

"I, erm, well, I think you might be expecting too much there," I mumbled, feeling myself blush scarlet.

Anna laughed. "It's about time," she said. "And it's certainly the first time Suzie's liked one of Marc's ladies enough to bring her out in public."

"Well it's the first time in years he's liked one enough to introduce me to her, " Suzie retorted. "Although to be fair, poor Jem has just been thrown on my mercy—there hasn't been much introducing going on."

"You'll be fine," Anna said to me. "I'm here with work," she explained. "I'm a television producer." She turned to Suzie. "Are you sitting with Mike and his darling witch of a wife?"

Suzie nodded. "I wish we weren't," she sighed. "A whole evening of listening to that cow crowing about her new car and holiday and interior fucking decor. All of it off the back of Black Swans. I swear they only encouraged Marc out of retirement in order to pay for her cosmetic surgery." She screwed her face up in distaste. "Come on," she said to me, "let's go and brave it." She grabbed two more glasses as we said our goodbyes to Anna, and then led me through the lobby in the direction of even louder noise.

We walked into what would normally have been a fairly average hotel function room, but which had been utterly transformed for the occasion. Dozens of circular tables creaked perilously under the weight of tall flower arrangements that were wedged against ice buckets jammed full with bottles of champagne. Tables of loud men in scruffy clothes yelled at each other over the heads of occasional groups of people in full evening dress. The waitresses appeared to have all been recruited from the Moulin Rouge and I wondered briefly if there were any naked waiters around to redress the balance. Suzie apparently knew exactly where we were heading, so I just followed meekly as she wriggled her way towards the front.

"Oh look, it's Marc's new pet!" The sneering voice came from behind me. I turned to see my taxi escort sitting with a gaggle of men at a table already covered with empty beer bottles.

Suzie rolled her eyes. "Ignore the delightful Angelica," she said, pulling me forward, "she's a complete bitch. Oh look, here's our table—aren't we the lucky ones?" She smiled brightly at the people already sitting there. Our companions were one of the groups who'd dressed up for the occasion, all the men trussed up in shiny suits and bow ties. The solitary woman amongst them was wearing a full length beaded dress topped with an overdose of glittering jewellery and a face that looked as though it might melt if she got too close to the lights.

"Mike," she nodded, "Wendy." The woman gave a tight, unfriendly smile.

"I'm not keen on journalists," Wendy said loudly. Her

husband smiled indulgently.

Mike leaned across the table to shake my hand. He felt clammy. "So you're the lucky new lady," Suzie pulled our chairs out and poked me into sitting down, immediately grabbing a full bottle out of the bucket on the table.

"I'm no one's anything," I said sharply. Mike raised an eyebrow and went back to talking to the man next to him without bothering to reply. I turned to Suzie. "Does everyone think I'm a fucking groupie?" I hissed.

"Of course not," she soothed. "Here, have another drink."

"And what's with that bloody woman bitching at me?" I asked, nodding towards the back of the hall, where the blonde from the taxi was still glaring at me over her drink. "Angelica? She's made it very clear that she doesn't like me." Suzie looked over my shoulder towards the back of the hall.

"Aah, yeah," Suzie said, draining her glass, "Angie hates you, on account of how she is clearly madly in love with darling Marc. She was the only one who'd speak to him for a while, during the rough times. It wasn't a relationship or anything like that," she continued quickly, seeing my expression, "I think she was just company when he was in the middle of what we like to call his 'lost weekend'. Went on for over a year, that weekend did." She sighed heavily at the memory. "Anyway," she said, topping up both our glasses, despite my attempts to wave her hand away, "Angie was convenient company, I guess. Paul says he feels sorry for her, just hanging around like a lost puppy all the time. But she's never quite given up on him. So no," she finished brightly, "Angie is never going to be your friend." I risked a brief peek behind me. Angie was ignoring the drunken chatter at her table in favour of staring at us. I turned back sharply and drained my glass in one move. Suzie happily refilled it. "God I hate these things," she confided. "It's so nice to have company."

"Don't the other wives and girlfriends ever come?" I asked.

Suzie snorted. "Kier's wife left him when she found out he'd gambled all the money away," she said. "I'm pretty sure Stef's still married to Zena, but she lives in the country raising their feral children and I haven't seen her for years."

"You have kids," I pointed out.

"Yes, but I've never let that spoil my fun," Suzie said. "My mum's always good for babysitting and Paul still likes going out occasionally. We don't cut loose very often, but when we do, we do it *properly*," she cackled. "Another drink?"

Most of the show passed by in a blur of famous faces who all seemed much smaller in real life. The room was getting increasingly rowdy and I'd taken to tipping my wine into a nearby plant pot at regular intervals so that I wouldn't end up completely hammered. Suzie clearly had no such concerns, waving and shouting to people she recognised and leaning across the table to take bottles out of the bucket right under Mike's nose, much to his wife's obvious disapproval.

"She should drink more, it might help her crack a smile," Suzie said to me, loudly enough for it to be heard across the table. "Wendy," she nodded and raised a bottle in salute, before giggling and slapping me on the leg. "Our heroes will be here any minute now," she informed me, peering at her watch. "Not that it's much of a surprise appearance." She looked around the room. "I reckon half the people here are just waiting for Marc to fall flat on his face. Literally, if at all possible. They want him to make a complete idiot of himself so that they can all say 'I told you so' in a judgmental fashion. Probably whilst snorting cocaine in the toilets. He'll show them." Suddenly

I felt nervous—for Marc, but also for me. I'd been having such fun with Suzie that I'd almost forgotten the real reason I was here. What if he didn't like me when he saw me again? More importantly, what if *I* didn't like *him*? But before I could think about it any more, there was a commotion as a boy band—whose enthusiastic performance had been roundly ignored by everyone present—exited the stage and were almost bowled over by the compere. I recognised him as the DJ from a national breakfast show, who bolstered his career by regularly popping up on various reality TV programmes. He came out onto the stage with a microphone in one hand and a bottle of beer in the other and, by the way he staggered slightly, I suspected that his radio stint would be something of a struggle the next morning.

"Ladies and gentlemen," he slurred, "I can only hope that they're more sober than I am. May I introduce our surprise guests—Black Swans!" The curtain dropped and there was Marc. I sucked a sharp breath and had to try my very hardest not to wriggle on my seat. As they ploughed into 'My Heart', Suzie leaned over.

"They've still got it," she said, gleeful satisfaction audible in her voice. I doubted anyone in the room could disagree, even if they wanted to. Marc was playing the crowd as if it was a tiny intimate gig, rather than a huge showbiz party. Jumping down off the stage, he prowled the tables, howling into the faces of record company execs and their flustered wives whilst the rest of Black Swans grinned at each other and thrashed through the music as though they'd never been away. Suddenly he was at our table. Wendy puffed up immediately, but before she could reach out to touch him, he turned his back on her and pressed up against me. He kept singing, but trailed a delicate hand down my neck as he did so. I tried not to die of embarrassed exposure as I became horribly aware that all the cameras were now pointing at me, whilst also feeling electricity shoot down my spine at Marc's touch. Then he was off again, springing lithely back onto the stage and leaving me sitting there, breathless. People at nearby tables stared curiously, but I was past caring. I picked up the nearest bottle and filled my glass, downing it in one just as Black Swans left the stage to rapturous applause.

"Well, that'll show people," said Suzie triumphantly, leaning over to me. "And boy, has Marc got the hots for *you*, young lady." I felt myself redden, then gave in to the inevitable.

"You really think so?"

Suzie looked at me as if I'd left my brain at the door. "Are you kidding?" she looked incredulous. "He's only met you once and already you're out in public with him. He wouldn't have even mentioned you to me if it had been a mistake, let alone asked me to bring you with me tonight."

"I'm worried that I just look like an amateur who can't keep her knickers on."

Suzie's face creased into a lopsided grin. "Oh Jem," she hooted, "you really need to leave some of your morals at the door." She waved her glass around at me. "Marc's not as much of a heartbreaker as his publicity would have you think. He doesn't just pull girls out of the crowd for an easy lay. He clearly wants you. And he usually gets what he wants." As the ceremony came to an end, people started to move around the room, loudly discussing which party they were heading off to. Someone I recognised as one of Black Swans' road crew approached me. He was younger than most of the others and looked gratifyingly friendly.

"Hey," he smiled. "Jem, right?" I nodded. "Marc asked me to give you this. See you later, yeah?" And with that he was off again, darting through the crowds towards the stage exit. I opened the folded piece of paper nervously. *'Embarrassment suits you. I'm looking forward to getting you alone later. M x'* Trying not to squeak like a lovesick teenager, I folded the paper back up and carefully zipped it into my jacket pocket. I looked up to see Suzie watching me.

"Told you, didn't I?" I said nothing, just stood there grinning like a lovesick idiot. "Right," she wobbled to her feet, "let's get out of here and go worship our conquering heroes." I picked up her handbag and she took it gratefully. "I like you, Jem," she announced, clutching my arm for support, "and I think Marc should keep you. I shall tell him that." Turning to the rest of the table she beamed and gave a thumbs up to Wendy. "Went well enough to pay for your colonic irrigation a for a while, eh, Wend?" Wendy turned puce and elbowed her husband, but he was deep in conversation with a blonde television actress and didn't pay her any attention.

Suzie laughed. "Come on, Jem," she said loudly, "the menfolk are waiting." I followed dutifully as she wove her way through the tables of drunken musicians and journalists, a couple of whom I vaguely recognised. A tall skinny dark woman caught my arm as we passed through and I had to grab Suzie before she disappeared into the crowd—I'd have no idea where to go and wasn't convinced of my blagging abilities. And I'd left my hotel room key in the bathroom, I realised with a sigh. Fixed grin applied, I turned to speak to the woman who'd stopped me. She looked vaguely familiar but I couldn't figure out why.

"Jemimah, isn't it?" she said in a friendly tone that didn't quite mask the sharpness underneath. "From that little newspaper out in the sticks."

"Who are you?" I snapped. Suzie came up beside me, all five foot of her preparing to jump to my defence. The woman raised a sharply arched eyebrow. "No need to be bad tempered, dear," she said. "You're Zoe's friend, aren't you? She and I work together." The penny finally dropped.

"Kate. You do the celebrity section."

She nodded. Bollocks. "I'm surprised to see you here, I must say," she said archly. "Didn't Zoe want to come?"

"Zoe doesn't know I'm here." Her eyebrow rose even higher. "It was a last minute invitation and I don't run everything past my friends."

"Of course not," she smiled sweetly. Fucking bitch. "I'm sure Zoe will be thrilled to see you in the papers, anyway. Maybe your boyfriend will keep the clippings. So," her eyes glinted slightly, "you and Gatton, then?"

"We need to go," said Suzie, tugging at my sleeve. I smiled as pleasantly as I could manage at Kate.

"Nice to see you again," I lied. "I'll be sure to keep an eye on the papers. Now if you don't mind, Marc's waiting for me." Leaving her staring after us in a very satisfying fashion, we shimmied through the crowd to a door at the side of the stage. A burly security guard eyed us suspiciously, and then smiled in recognition.

"Aah, the ladies," he grinned, holding the door open. "Evening, girls. I must say your blokes were bloody good tonight. I'm a big fan." He wedged himself between us and a group of teenagers who were clearly angling to get in. "You have fun now." With that the door shut behind us and we were left in a long service corridor.

"It's okay, I know where we're going," Suzie declared confidently, wobbling off ahead of me. "We head for the noise." I wasn't convinced, but sure enough sounds of people and clinking glasses came from a doorway further down. Suzie pulled open a pair of swing doors and ushered me into a large conference room that had been done up for a party. The air was thick and warm and the noise headache inducing as I stepped over several people sprawled on the floor. It was becoming a recurrent theme. Mike and Wendy were already holding court in a corner of the room and Suzie led us determinedly to a bar at the opposite end.

"Two *very* large gin and tonics, darling," she said to the barman, and then turned to me. "These events are what make me drink," she declared loudly. "All the band hate them, but they have to turn up like good little cash-cows. Aah," she waved over my shoulder, "there's Paul, thank fuck." I turned slowly, almost dreading looking Marc in the eye again but also squirming with excitement. I struggled to hide my disappointment when I realised Paul was alone.

He grinned when he saw me. "Hey Jem," he leant forward for a hug and kissed me enthusiastically on the cheek. "So great that you could come. Marc's held up with another interview, he'll be here as soon as he can manage. Sweetheart," he kissed Suzie, "please can we leave straight away? I'd rather sit with your mother and the kids than stay in this pit of vipers."

"Wow, and I thought it was only me who didn't appreciate Wendy's hospitality," she replied with a roll of her eyes. "Yeah, gimme a sec to finish this." She downed her drink and I wondered how she hadn't fallen over. "This bar," she declared to me with a delicate hiccup, "is free. Which means the boys are paying for it. I am relying on you to drink our share, just to piss Wendy off."

"On my own?" I could hear the desperation in my own voice.

Suzie patted my arm. "You'll be fine," she said. "Marc will be here soon and you can get happily sloshed in the meantime. You'll look after her, won't you—" she squinted at the barman's name-tag "—Gabriel?"

Gabriel nodded keenly. "Oh yes", he said, "any friend of Marc Gatton's is a friend of mine. Big fan." Was there anyone here who *wasn't* a bloody fan of Marc's? I hoisted myself up onto a bar stool and tried not to look too far out of my depth as Suzie and Paul left me to my fate.

"Another drink, Jem?" Gabriel—"Call me Gabe!"—had long ago decided that we were friends. And I'd long ago hit the point where I just wanted to go home. Perhaps I could collect my things from the room and get the night bus. Or, more sensibly, I could stay in my luxury suite and see how many room service charges I could make Marc pay for. I checked my watch—forty minutes since Suzie and Paul had left. It felt much longer. I'd spotted Wendy peering at me more than once with a superior smile on her face that was making me feel murderous. Murderous and foolish. I decided that enough was enough—fuck Marc Gatton, I was going to leave. I slid down from my bar stool and stumbled slightly. Gabe reached over the bar to steady my arm.

"Actually I think I'd like a glass of water," I said, and propped myself back onto the stool. I needed to clear my head before I had to face the walk of shame back through the room and out into the night. Alone. Hot angry tears pricked at the back of my eyes. How fucking dare Marc leave me hanging around like this? I might not be the sort of glamour puss he was clearly used to, but I was better than this, for fuck's sake. Righteous anger sobered me up slightly and I stood up again to leave just as there was a commotion at the door.

"Your man's here, Jem," grinned Gabe. "He's a one, isn't he?" I turned round. Marc was walking across the room, peering around as though he was looking for someone. The crowd was too cool to show any excitement at seeing him, but the murmuring intensified and eyes focused on his every move, even as they pretended to be carrying on their conversations. He spotted me when he was halfway across the room and the sudden grin on his face melted any worries I might have had. Loping over to the bar, he scooped me up and swung me round as I clung to his neck like a monkey. Marc turned to Gabe, who was staring at the pair of us with a look of soppy adoration on his face.

"Thanks for looking after her, mate. She's precious, this one." He slipped a note across the bar.

"My pleasure," said Gabe, pocketing the cash smoothly. "You've done well there," he nodded towards me, "mind you hang onto her."

"Oh I have every intention of doing so," said Marc. "Literally." I squirmed at the intent look in his eye. "Shall we go, Jem?" I nodded. Marc picked up my bag from the bar and wedged it under his arm. "Suits me, I think" he winked. He pulled me swiftly through the room, nodding and smiling at people as he went and determinedly avoiding Wendy, who was waving and beckoning him over to her in a proprietorial fashion. Her face tightened as she saw me and I couldn't resist smiling sweetly. Once through the door, Marc tugged my arm. "Come on," he said urgently, breaking out into a run in the corridor. I let myself be towed along, laughing and stumbling as we went. Marc pulled me sharply through a small doorway into an empty room.

"Fucking hell, Jem," he gasped, closing the door behind us and pushing me up against it. His hands were all over me—grabbing my hair and running down my back, pulling me hard against him. I clung to him, groaning as he kissed and bit my neck, his hands sliding up inside my dress. Suddenly he pulled away and grinned. "Look," he said gleefully, sliding his hand into his trouser pocket, "I went to the chemist like a teenager." He held out a handful of condoms.

"What if someone had recognised you?" I laughed. "And you're not telling me you've had those in your pocket all evening? What if they'd fallen out whilst you were on stage?"

"Who gives a shit?" he said, "'*middle-aged man practises safe sex*' isn't much of a headline, is it? Anyway, I've got more important things to worry about." He reached round me and wedged a broom up against the door handle. I fumbled for his belt, tugging it undone and pulling frantically at his zip. I slipped a hand inside his trousers and felt him hard and throbbing against my palm. Without thinking, I sank to my knees and took him in my mouth, tasting the salty warmth of his flesh as he moaned and clutched at my hair.

"Jesus," he muttered, "I'm going to come right now if you carry on." He pulled back and looked down at me. "You are something else, you know that?" I just grinned at him, all thoughts of the outside world gone from my mind. Right now, all that mattered was that I had him standing in front with the most ridiculously lascivious expression on his face. It's the simple pleasures that matter in life, after all. Marc pulled me to my feet and turned me round so I had my back to him.

"Bend over that," he instructed, pushing me towards a stack of boxes in the corner of the room, "and lift your skirt up.

There's a good girl." He winked, which would have been cute had he not also been gripping his rock hard erection at the same time. Dropping my jacket onto the floor, I did as I was told, bending over the boxes and slowly sliding my skirt up around my waist. There was complete silence for a second during which I nearly lost my nerve and stood up, but then I felt Marc's hand on me. I heard the rustle of foil and then he was up against me, pressing insistently between my legs. "Open up for me, Jem," he muttered. I wriggled and spread my legs slightly, my eyes tight shut and my hands gripping the edge of the box. Without another word, Marc sank deep inside me, a hand sliding round and feeling for me as he pushed tight up against me. "Christ you feel so good," he murmured. "I'm not going to last long." I mumbled something about not caring and pushed back against him, needing to feel him hard inside me, fucking me as if it was the only thing on earth that he wanted. He gave up any pretence of gentleness and slammed against me, fucking me like a rag doll as I gritted my teeth and shifted so that his hand was pressed against me as he moved, waves of sensation building up deep inside me and making me cry out as I felt him swell inside me, stretching me open and making me take everything he could give, my entire body off the floor and slumped over the boxes as he fucked me and took me and made me shriek with want and need. "Jesus...fucking hell Jem...so good..." he lost control entirely, spasming against me just as I hit my own peak and wailed aloud at the incredible waves that were crashing over me and turning my insides molten. He thrashed against me and I shrieked as I felt him explode, pulsing hard against my tightening muscles. We leaned over the boxes together as we caught our breath, Marc still deep inside me and gasping incoherently. Eventually we both straightened up and leaned back against the walls as we caught our breath. I could feel sweat dripping onto my back and every muscle in my body ached from the tension. I noticed a mop bucket next to his feet and laughed.

He turned to look at me. "Funny, am I?"

I grinned back at him as I stood amidst boxes of disinfectant with my dress rucked up around my waist. "Just general amazement," I reassured him. "Who'd have ever thought that a drunken fuck in a cleaning cupboard could turn out to be one of the most spectacular experiences of my life?"

Marc grinned, standing there with his trousers still undone and clearly not giving a shit. "Of your entire life?" I nodded and he looked thoroughly pleased with himself. "Then I'm not an entirely washed up old idiot just yet."

"You've never been that," I protested.

Marc grinned. "My ex wife might disagree with you there," he said. "But I'm glad you enjoy getting naked with me, because I sure as hell like doing it with you. In fact," he said, pulling me close, "I think you should come back to my hotel room and do an awful lot more of it. Just to make sure."

LET'S GO TO BED

S o anyway, if you've never had furiously passionate, spur of the moment sex with someone you've fantasised about for pretty much all your adult life, then I'm here to highly recommend it as a pastime. After we'd scrabbled our clothes together and Marc had wiped my face and tucked my hair behind my ears "…so that you don't look *entirely* as though you've just been fucked senseless", we managed to make our escape through the back corridors of the hotel and up to the top floor.

"Aren't we going to your room?" I asked in surprise, as Marc headed towards my suite.

He looked at me with what was rapidly becoming a very familiar grin. "This *is* my room," he replied. "Or rather, it's *our* room—it's booked in both names. I'm not assuming anything though," he continued hurriedly, "I've already arranged with Paul and Suzie that I'll go in with them if you'd rather sleep alone."

"That's very…thoughtful," I said, trying not to laugh, "but I'm cool with sharing."

"Lucky me," grinned Marc, his green eyes twinkling. "Angie should have dropped my stuff off after you left—I warned her not to unpack it, in case I wasn't staying." He opened the door with a keycard from his own pocket. A small but expensive-looking leather suitcase now sat on the bed. I headed into the bathroom to inspect what was left of my makeup and stopped short. Male toiletries were laid out on the shelf alongside a brown leather wash bag and my own collection of lovely bathroom things had been unceremoniously decanted into the waste bin. Marc heard my squeak of indignation and came into the bathroom behind me, groaning slightly as he realised what had happened. "Bloody hell," he muttered, "she doesn't help herself."

I turned to face him. "It's fine," I said, "nothing's been damaged." Marc didn't look convinced. I tried to sound casual as I picked things up. "Is there any reason that Angie's so…protective?"

Marc sighed. "It's a long story," he said, "and some of it isn't my business to tell. Angie sees me as, well…" Marc looked uncomfortable as he trailed off, "…as a father figure, I guess. She's loyal and protective and sometimes she takes things a bit too far. I'll have words with her."

I straightened up and looked him in the eye. "Why does she have such an issue with me, Marc?" I asked. "What is it we're actually doing? Because I need to know. Are we—am I—just temporary fuck-buddies? Because I'm not sure I can do that. Your…*friends* are getting ideas—some of them more flattering than others—and at some point I'm going to have to go home and face the person who still thinks he's my boyfriend. My *boyfriend*, Marc!" It occurred to me that it was the first time I'd said his name to his face—I'd been avoiding it before, I had no idea why. Perhaps it was just too intimate. He stepped forward and gripped my arms. His eyes were tight and I could see the creases in the corners. He looked tired.

"Honestly, Jem?" His eyes bored into mine and I forced myself not to look away. "You want to know honestly what I think?" I nodded silently. He dropped my arms and gave me a tired smile. "I have absolutely no fucking idea what this is all about. I don't really know how it happened and I sure as hell don't know where it's going." Even as my heart sank and I felt sick to the stomach, he reached out to stroke my cheek. "What I *do* know is that I like you, a lot," I genuinely felt my heart lurch at that, "and I would very much like it if we could keep seeing each other. We're good together, don't you think?" I hesitated, and then nodded silently. "But," he continued, "the honest answer is that I just don't know." I could see our joint reflection in the bathroom mirror in the corner of my eye and had a flash of just how bizarre this all was. I was standing in a hotel bathroom, discussing feelings and emotions with Marc Gatton. But he wasn't the rock star from my teenage posters any more—he was just Marc. Marc, standing in front of me looking like nothing more than a normal, vulnerable bloke who didn't know what the fuck was happening.

"Well I'm glad you don't know what you're doing," I said, deciding to meet his honestly head-on, "because neither do I. You were supposed to be *work*. But now I'm overstepping boundaries and betraying my partner and potentially risking friendships, all because I clearly have no self control." Marc laughed at that and stepped forward to touch me, but I put up my hand. "No, let me finish. I might just be a suburban hack," he frowned and looked as if he was about to say something, but stopped himself, "but I *like* my job. I like living out of town and I like that I know roughly what every week will hold before it starts. But now I *don't* know, and it's confusing me. Because this isn't meant to happen, Marc. People in my position don't just end up in bed with rock stars. Or rather," I corrected myself, remembering some of Zoe's more exotic teenage escapades, "they do, but they don't expect it to be anything more than a one night stand. And this," I waved my arms around vaguely, "is a bit more than a one-off. Even if we never see each other again," Marc frowned, "you made it publicly clear tonight that I was with you. You sang at me on camera, for heaven's sake!" He laughed at that. "People *saw*, Marc," I continued. "People who know me personally saw it. Everyone witnessed it." *And if Kate has anything to do with it she will get a story out of it*, I thought to myself. "I'm already lying to my oldest, closest friend and I've known you for what," I shrugged, "not quite two days?"

"It seems so much longer," Marc mused, then looked me directly in the eye. "Have you really had to lie about me?" I nodded and he looked concerned.

"I haven't had any choice," I pointed out. "I've behaved like an absolute asshole and need to sort things out with Dan because it's the least I owe him. And I don't want anyone else to know for the simple reason that it's none of their business and you're too important to gossip about." Marc looked at me, a quizzical expression in his grey eyes.

"So does that mean you like me?"

I sighed and rolled my eyes. "Of course I do!" I blurted. "You're funny and amazingly attractive and absolutely astonishingly good in bed. Even though we haven't actually made it *into* a bed yet," he blushed at that. "And I am already very fond of you. But until I work out where I stand, I don't know how I feel about any of it. So the last thing I want to do is to let other people in on my secret. Although," I sighed, "I suspect that this evening's performance has taken that one out of my hands."

"Well it'll give them all something to think about," grinned Marc. "And it's nice for Suzie to have someone to hang out with. She likes you."

"I like her, too," I said. "Very much. But I'm well aware that if this," I waved my hands vaguely around us both, "goes belly up, then I won't see her anymore."

Marc caught my arm and pulled me towards him, wrapping his arms tight around me with his head buried in my neck. "Suzie won't let you go," he said. "Not even if I do. But I don't think I will." He pulled back slightly and looked me in the eye. "I rather like being around you. You're good for me, Jemimah Holliday."

"And I'm pretty sure you're just a bad influence on me," I retorted. Marc's eyes twinkled, but I could see the exhaustion in them. "Come on," I said, tugging him out of the bathroom, "let's go to bed. And sleep. Like normal people."

"You're such a bully," laughed Marc, but he allowed himself to be pulled towards the bed. "And I can't promise that I will keep my hands to myself all night. But I would very much like to curl up with you right now."

"Good," I said, "you look fit to drop." He sat on the edge of the bed, kicking off his shoes as I moved his case onto the floor so that I could sit beside him. Standing up, he wriggled out of his trousers and unbuttoned the shirt that was still damp with sweat. He frowned slightly as he peeled it off.

"Can you bear it if I don't shower right now?" he asked. "I'm fucking knackered."

"It's fine," I reassured him. "Teenage me would be wetting her knickers with excitement even if you stank like a drain. Which you don't," I hurriedly added.

Marc grinned. "You make me feel very old sometimes," he said. "Although I don't actually know how old you are, which is rather remiss of me."

"Thirty," I informed him. "Practically ancient."

Marc leaned back on the pillows, patting the space next to him encouragingly. "Well I've got a couple of decades on you," he said. "I'm forty nine next birthday. Old enough to know better," he gave a wry smile. "I should have given up on all this years ago. But somehow I just can't seem to let it go." He grinned. "And nights like this certainly help make it all worthwhile." He pulled idly at the hem of my dress. "Isn't it time you got undressed?" He had a frankly libidinous grin on his face and I blushed. There was something far more intimate about taking my clothes off intentionally than when they were just being ripped off and thrown on the floor. Marc raised a silently expectant eyebrow. I bent down to unlace my boots, then stood up with my back to him and kicked them off. Ugh, I'd forgotten I was wearing thick socks to stop my boots rubbing. Bending over, I pulled them off quickly and shoved them into my bag.

"That's a very pleasant view," said Marc. "Although I'll be happier when the rest of it's off as well." I kept my back to him in the hope that my blushes would have faded before he noticed. At least I was wearing decent underwear, for a change. I pulled the dress over my head in one quick movement and threw it towards my bag in the corner of the room, then wriggled out of my bra. God only knows what had happened to my knickers—I strongly suspected that a cleaner was going to get a surprise when they next ventured into the broom cupboard. For someone who usually lived a very boring life, I'd taken very easily to leaving knickers in random strange rooms. Taking a deep breath, I turned to face Marc and discovered him grinning like a cat who'd not only got the cream, but had been handed the keys to the entire dairy.

"Oh yes," he murmured, "nights like this make *everything* better." He held his arms out. "But I'm worn out and too far over the hill to go for a second run just yet. Come and curl up with me." I climbed onto the bed and Marc pulled me against him, my head nestling into his shoulder. "This is nice," he murmured. I was suddenly exhausted now that the alcohol and the excitement of the evening were wearing off. I mumbled something incoherent in return and snuggled into the warmth of him. As I drifted off with his arms around me, I dared to imagine falling asleep like this all the time. Maybe I could.

SOME DAYS ARE JUST A BAG OF DICKS

I woke up to light coming in through hotel curtains and a cold space beside me. Rolling over, I discovered Marc sitting on the edge of the bed, frowning at his phone as he typed a message. I slid a hand up his back and he turned to look at me with a distracted smile.

"Morning," he said. "You slept well."

"Mmmm," was all I could manage at the sight of him naked in my bed. My hand slid down to his thigh, hopeful of a morning wake up call.

Marc gave a short laugh and wriggled away. "I need to get going," he said. To my surprise, he got up off the bed and started picking up his clothes. "Something's come up that I need to sort out. You'll be okay to see yourself out? It's all paid for." Taken aback, I didn't say anything. I sat clutching the crisp white bed sheets round my knees as I watched Marc getting ready to leave. He walked swiftly around the room picking things up and throwing them into his bag as a coldness settled in my stomach. All the intimacy of the previous night was gone and his jaw was rigid with tension.

"Is it," I didn't know where to start. "Is it something I said?"

Marc stopped and sighed. "I told you I wasn't expecting anything," I continued.

He came over to the bed and smiled down at me, but the smile didn't quite reach his eyes. "It's all good," he said, in what was clearly intended to be a reassuring tone, but failed miserably. He dropped a card on the bed. "My number. Let's catch up again soon." Bending over, he kissed the top of my head and picked up his bags in one movement. "Take care, Jem." With that, he turned for the door and left without with another word.

I sat there on the bed for a very long time, frozen with shock. *Let's catch up.* So it clearly had meant nothing to him, even after everything he'd said. Just a good line in smooth talk in order for him to indulge in a fling, probably one of hundreds. What a fucking idiot I'd been. I threw off the covers and got out of bed in a cold, sick fury. There was a square of white card on the floor—the one he'd dropped on the bed as he left—and I bent to pick it up. It turned out to be a business card from a Thai restaurant in the West End. On the back was scribbled 'MG' and a phone number. I couldn't quite bring myself to throw it in the bin, so I found my overnight bag and shoved the card inside one of my sweaty socks from the night before. I went into the bathroom and switched on the shower, climbing in and turning the water up as hot as I could bear. I washed every inch of myself and rubbed at my hair with hotel-issue shampoo, desperately trying to make myself feel clean again. *Let's catch up.* Ugh. Wrapping myself in a towel, I scooped up the toiletries that I'd rescued the previous night and decanted them back into the waste bin, wondering as I did so how many women Suzie had shopped for in the past. The silver dress I'd been so pleased with was crumpled in a heap on the floor—I picked it up and shoved it into my bag like an old rag. Putting on the same clothes I'd worn for work the previous day, I realised with a grimace that they were now going into their third day of wear. I rescued the perfume yet again and doused myself in the hope of smelling less musty, then dropped the heavy glass bottle into my bag as a miserable souvenir. In the cold light of day, the excitement of the awards ceremony seemed like something from a different world. Jamming bare feet into my battered boots, I scanned the room for anything I'd forgotten. The sight of the bed still crumpled from where Marc and I had curled up together made my eyes prickle and I gave myself a shake. *Just mark it down to experience*, I told myself. I knew I'd still do it again, even if I could go back in time. I looked at my phone and was surprised to discover that it still wasn't quite 8am. It must have been quite some emergency to get him going so early. I remembered how weary he'd seemed the night before—the soft and kind Marc that I'd fallen asleep with was a completely different person to the impersonal man who'd walked out of the hotel an hour ago. Slinging my bag over my shoulder, I banged out of the hotel room door and slammed it behind me with far more force than was necessary. In order to avoid other people I took the staircase down to the lobby and breathed deeply before I pushed through the doors into the reception.

The woman behind the desk gave me a blindingly white smile as I approached. "Mr Gatton had to leave early, I gather? That's a shame," she said. I gritted my teeth, but there didn't seem to be anything more than friendly curiosity in her eyes.

"Always busy, you know how it is," I replied in as calm a voice as I could manage and she nodded. "I need to check out," I added, rather unnecessarily.

81

She peered at the screen in front of her and tapped at her keyboard, before looking back up at me. "All taken care of," she said with a friendly smile. "Perhaps we'll see you both again soon?" I was saved having to answer by someone calling my name across the lobby. Turning, I saw Suzie heading out of the lift towards me. Behind her was Paul, who was helping an older woman herd two small children and carrying a ridiculous amount of luggage. The last thing I needed right now was happy families. I put a hand up in vague acknowledgment and stalked out, leaving Suzie staring after me from the middle of the hotel reception as I pushed my way out onto the street. I gritted my teeth and switched my phone back on—it began pinging with missed text messages before I'd got even halfway down the road. I stopped to scrabble round in my bag for it and was completely unsurprised to find that it was Zoe.

"What the fuck? You owe me an explanation, lady!" I was already late for work—maybe I should make the most of being in town and get it over with. Tris would be cross at having to wait for the gossip, but he'd live. I sent him a quick message. *"I need to sort some things out. Tell Arthur I'll be in later."* I was up to date with my commissions for the Mercury—so long as I got the article in before the printers' weekly deadline, they could hardly complain. I called Zoe as I headed towards the tube station sign I could see in the distance.

She picked it up before it had even started ringing at my end. "Where are you and why did I not know about you and Mr Loverman?" she shrieked through the ether. I held my phone away from my ear slightly.

"Calm down, Zo," I said. "It's not as interesting as it seems. I mean—obviously it is, but…" I trailed off.

"Are you still in town?" she asked. "Can you meet me in

Soho in half an hour? Usual place?" I stopped outside the tube station to look for my travel card. Several people bumped into me, grumbling as I juggled the phone and my bag. I took refuge in the doorway of a boarded up shop.

"Yes, I'll come find you," I sighed. "Let the inquisition begin."

Zoe was already settled into a corner booth of her favourite coffee shop when I arrived, belongings spilling across the bench beside her. Zoe herself also spilled everywhere. She always had done, somehow taking up more space than she actually occupied through sheer force of nature. My oldest and dearest friend was undeniably gorgeous in a slightly feral way—all curves and lips and sweeps of long black hair, which today were set off by a luxuriant fake fur leopard print coat. Zoe would have gone down a storm in the fifties, but these days she just looked brilliantly off-kilter in the bony world of fashion and television that she inhabited.

"You secretive fucking bitch!" she squawked as I pushed through the door, causing heads to turn briefly before deciding I wasn't all that exciting and going back to their lattes. I slumped down opposite her just as a very attractive barista came over to take our order.

"Black Americano," I said. "Extra shot, please."

He grinned. "Good night, was it?" he said with a grin.

Zoe narrowed her eyes. "It clearly was," she said, glaring at me. "And I am expecting some serious gossip to make up for having been left out of this particular storyline." I sighed and waited until the barista was safely back behind the counter. Groaning, I leant backwards and stretched my neck over the back of the seat, feeling my spine click most satisfyingly.

"It wasn't intended, if that helps," I said. "He invited me and

83

it would have been silly not to go. It's as simple as that. We're friends." Zoe was silent so I sat forward again. She was staring at me as if she wasn't sure whether to laugh or shout.

"You're friends with Dracula now?" She poked a sharply pointed, blood-red fingernail in my direction. "You have teeth marks on your neck, for chrissakes!" The barista turned up with my coffee, his eyes widening with interest. My hand automatically shot up to my neck as he put down my mug and then started wiping a neighbouring table without even having the grace to pretend that he wasn't eavesdropping. I felt myself blush as I pulled out my phone and used the camera to inspect my neck. I did indeed appear to have what looked horribly like a love bite just above my left collarbone. I swore quietly to myself and Zoe leant across the table.

"Come on then," she said, "tell me all about it before I burst!"

I decided to be honest. "It was brilliant," I grinned. "I mean, it was good the first time, but almost nicer the second—what?"

Zoe was staring at me wide eyed. "This has happened *twice*? You hadn't even met him when I spoke to you on Monday! It is now," she thought for a second, "yes, it's still only Wednesday. And you've had Gatton in the sack twice already?" She hunched down as I frantically shushed her—heads were beginning to turn and I was desperately hoping that the sort of people who came into this coffee shop were far too cool to do anything as bourgeois as watching television.

I stirred my coffee intently in order to avoid her gaze. "Well we didn't get as far as bed the first time," I ignored her choking snorts, "and the second time we *did* get into bed—eventually—but it was romantic rather than hot. Well, it was hot first and then romantic afterwards. And then it all went a bit weird, to be honest."

"Well, of course it did," she said. I looked up to see her flicking through images on her iPad. "Renowned twat, is Gatton. Refuses to speak to journalists, doesn't drink at parties, just sits in the corner with his mate Paul. Glares at people a lot. Seen this?" She held the iPad screen up to show me an article from one of the major news websites. A photo showed him striding between the tables at the Saturn Awards, the rest of the band nothing more than a blur on the stage behind him. A second photo showed him singing directly at a woman with tousled blonde hair and a wicked look in her black-ringed eyes. Oh god, it was me. Really me. In the papers with a man who was absolutely not my boyfriend. I groaned as Zoe chortled gleefully. "Look," she said, reaching over the table to grip my hand for emphasis, "it's about time you remembered how to have fun. And you certainly didn't do it by halves." She snorted again and leant over to flick to another photograph, this time of Marc leaning against me and singing with his hand resting on my neck. I was staring straight at the camera, a very unflattering red blush creeping up my neck. Suzie was in the corner of the frame, appearing to slap my leg whilst spilling champagne everywhere from her other hand.

"You'd like Suzie," I said weakly.

Zoe snorted. "I know Suzie Fisher," she said, "we've run into each other in the past. Let's just say she needs to learn to wind her neck in when she's had a few." Zoe peered at me through her long fake lashes. "So, when are you seeing lover boy again?"

I shrugged. "There's nothing going on, Zo." She looked unconvinced. "We had fun, that's all. There's vague plans to catch up again some time, but nothing else."

She sat back in her seat. "Well I'm disappointed in you,

Jemimah Holliday," she said. "All this years of planning what you'd do with Marc Gatton, and the minute you actually *get* him, you let him slip through your fingers."

I bristled. "If you must know," I blurted, "he was bloody lovely but then it all went weird and now I don't have a bloody clue where I stand. Probably nowhere. So I'm very sorry if I let you down."

Zoe looked taken aback for a second, and then rallied. "Okay, okay," she soothed, her hand reaching for mine across the table. It would have been more comforting had she not been wearing her usual half dozen oversized rings, all of which scratched horribly. "So, you had fun and then he turned out to be just like the rest of them. Why don't you tell me all about it and I'll get it into this week's edition? It'd be great for me to get the exclusive lowdown and you'd get paid enough to have a nice holiday away from it all whilst Dan calms his man-tits."

I look at her in horror. "What the fuck?" My voice had gone up an octave and people on the nearby tables turned to look. I lowered my voice, but it took a lot of effort. "You think I'd sell my story?" I hissed at her, "the whole two days of it?" She shrugged. "Sometimes I wonder if you even know me at all," I muttered into my coffee.

Zoe was unperturbed. "Shit happens, Jem," she said levelly, circling the top of her espresso cup with the tip of her sharply manicured finger. "I'm just trying to make the best of it for you, that's all. For all of us." I glared at her. "At least think about it?"

"I've thought about it already," I said standing up. "The answer's no. I'm not for sale and neither is Marc Gatton. Whatever happens." People were openly staring now; I could see a woman at a corner table trying not to look too obvious as she took out her phone and snapped a photo of me glaring down at Zoe. "I'm going to work," I said, as much to the room at large as to Zoe. Fuck them all. "Call me when you remember how to act like a decent human being." I stalked out into the street and headed back to the safety of the tube, leaving Zoe gaping after me like a fish out of water.

RISE OF THE IDIOTS

I wasn't going to get past Tris without an inquisition, I knew that much. I gritted my teeth and pushed through the front doors into the Mercury's reception, but was pleasantly surprised to find him trapped behind his desk by a woman who was leaning over and lecturing him only inches from his face, her many chins wobbling indignantly as she spoke.

"My Waffles has been missing for over a week now and I want another appeal put into your paper," she was saying. "That's what local papers are for, isn't it—helping local people? What's the point in me paying my taxes for local services when we don't get any help when we need it? I pay your wages, young man." The smile that Tristan had pasted on his face was faltering, despite his obvious efforts.

"I really am sorry," he said politely, "and I do hope that Waffles comes home soon." The woman didn't budge. "But the Mercury isn't run by the council, so taxes have nothing to do with it. We've already mentioned your cat once and I can't force them to print things if there isn't a story in it."

"Of course there's a story," she retorted indignantly. "Everyone loves cats! The public would be horrified if they knew how unhelpful you were being. What if my Waffles is stuck somewhere and can't get home?" Tris saw me come through the door and frantically signaled for help as I walked past.

"Excuse me," he said to the woman. "Jem! Can you help this lady? Oh and we need to have that meeting we were talking about—you know, for you to fill me in on the current situation." I wasn't falling for that one. I stalked straight past, ducking sideways to avoid the woman who was now looking eagerly at me in the hope of support.

"Sorry Tris," I said, heading through the door into the main office, "got a million things to catch up with. I'm sure you're more than capable of helping this lovely lady find her Waffles." And with the brightest of smiles, I left him to his fate.

One of the joys of working for a tiny local paper was that there was often hardly any other staff around to annoy me. Arthur was nowhere to be seen and Neil, the main features writer, was away on holiday for the entire week. The only people currently in the office were Steph, who was in charge of advertising and thought of nothing but her allotment, Simon from accounts, who had an office of his own in the corner of the room (inside of which Tris had recently begun to spend a suspicious amount of time) and Geoff, who had been the chief (for which, read 'only') news reporter for more than twenty years and was consistently unaware of anything that happened outside a five mile radius of the office. He swung round towards me on his chair as I walked into the room.

"I see you made your television debut last night, Jem." *Shit.* Steph looked up, her eyes widening as she saw me.

"Oh Jem," she squawked excitedly, "tell us all about it! Did they have drink and drugs all over the place?" She tilted her head sympathetically. "You should be careful," she continued, "you know what those showbiz types are like." I slumped at my desk with a sigh.

"I'm not a showbiz type," I said. "And I didn't get drunk." Well, not *too* drunk. "I was invited, so I went. I thought it would be fun." I trailed off and stared blankly at my computer screen as it slowly booted itself up.

"You're not telling me it *wasn't* fun?" Geoff chortled. "We all saw you and that lady you were with, bouncing around like teenyboppers." Geoff was the only person I knew who would call adult women 'teenyboppers.' "And that man, whatshisname, the druggy rock star bloke, he was all over you like a rash! You mind what you're doing with that sort, lovey." It might have been nearly lunchtime but it was still way too early in the day for this crap. I made a show of pulling earphones out of my bag.

"The man's name is Marc," I said, pushing the ear buds in one at a time. "And whatever it looked like last night, he's just a friend. Not even a close one." That didn't seem like a lie after the events of this morning. "I promise I won't make a habit of turning up on television. Now if you don't mind, I have to get on with some work." They both looked disappointed as I swung away from them to stare at my desk, wondering where to start.

I wrote reviews all the time—five hundred words about how the local amateur dramatics group had really worked wonders with Pirates of Penzance this year, or a critique about whether the male voice choir should stick to singing words they understood, rather than attempting to barge their way through Land of My Fathers in the original Welsh just because one of them had cousins in Llanelli. We did occasionally get big names in town—mostly doing practice runs before they risked the London crowds—but the vast majority were of the type that my mum would have liked, rather than being anywhere near my taste. Although, I decided, Mum would probably have liked Black Swans. And she'd have definitely recognised Marc's appeal. I remembered how I used to sit on the stairs to watch her going out for her regular Friday night jolly with the girls from the office. She always looked much younger than the others, despite them all being about the same age. Mum never seemed to age at all in my eyes. Which had made it even more of a shock when the skin cancer that she'd had successfully treated years earlier came back with such a vengeance that by the time it was discovered, it was too late to do anything other than make the best of what time we had left. Six weeks was all we'd had. Six measly, too-short weeks between us finding out and her death, lying thin and quiet in a bleached white bed in the local hospice. Typically she'd spent most of that time making arrangements, because my mother was nothing if not pragmatic.

"Come on Jem," she'd said kindly, after finding me sobbing on the back doorstep one day soon after we got the news, "this sort of thing doesn't only happen to other people, you know. It just *happens*. Let's make the most of things and not let what time I've got left be filled with tears." It didn't stop me crying, but after that I only did it when she wasn't around. Dad and I followed her instructions mutely, from writing down the dictated list of distant relatives—most of whom neither of us even knew—who would need to be notified of her death, to the songs she wanted playing at her funeral. Actually it was just one song—an old eighties tune that was apparently big when she and dad had met. She told me to pick some others myself—"after all, I won't be able to hear them"—and I did so,

91

numbly accepting the funeral director's kindly suggestions as to what were popular hymns for 'younger people', despite none of us being religious and the service being held in the local crematorium. I'd sat through it in silence, holding dad's hand on one side and Zoe's on the other. Zoe had insisted on us both wearing full black with veils and dramatic makeup because 'your mum would have liked that'. I hadn't had the strength to argue that, actually, I was pretty sure that Mum wouldn't have given a shit if I'd turned up at the service wearing my pyjamas. Even if I'd have been capable of crying through the numbness I wouldn't have dared, for fear of getting panda eyes from dripping eyeliner. We somehow got through the service—even the bit when the curtain had clanked awkwardly closed around the coffin and Dad's hand gripped mine fractionally tighter for a brief second—and made it to the wake, where Dad was immediately swept off into a corner by endless sorrowful relatives that he hadn't seen in years.

We'd gone into town that night, Zoe and I, and I got the drunkest I'd ever been in my life. I threw up in an alleyway in Camden whilst Zoe stumbled around behind me, mumbling encouraging words about 'getting it all out' and woke up with a hangover that lasted three days. At a loss as to what else to do, I returned to work within a week and dad went back to his garden. He'd taken up with Jill within six months and I never once resented him for it. She'd been a school friend of mum's who'd lost touch, but cared enough to turn up to the funeral. She'd then taken it upon herself to keep an eye on dad in the weeks and months afterwards and it had genuinely helped. So I hadn't been remotely surprised when I turned up to visit without warning him one weekend and found Jill in the kitchen, wearing nothing except Dad's dressing gown.

He'd looked sheepish as he answered the door. "I, erm, I mean love…" he'd stuttered, as I looked past him and took in Jill's pink face as she was caught in the terrible act of making a cup of tea. I'd just patted him on the arm, told him it was fine and walked through to the kitchen, leaving Dad floundering in the hallway.

"Is there enough in the kettle for a coffee, Jill?" I'd asked, ignoring her flapping. "I'm gasping." I'd made small talk for half an hour whilst dad turned increasingly puce, then left without once mentioning the new situation. From then on, Jill was always at the house when I called and eventually she gave up making a pretence of ever leaving. She and dad had bought Pudding as a cute fluffy puppy a year or so later and they'd lived as a happy threesome ever since. Jill wouldn't like Black Swans. She'd smile kindly and say I must do whatever made me happy and genuinely mean it, but she wouldn't understand like I knew Mum would. Mum would have had a wicked twinkle in her eye. And she'd have known exactly why the thought of never seeing Marc again was so gut-clenchingly terrifying.

I spent most of the day catching up with run of the mill stuff—editing a couple of pieces I'd already written and collating submissions for that week's 'Letters to the Editor' section. You quickly learned to be a jack-of-all-trades when you worked on a paper as small as the Mercury. By four in the afternoon, I'd done everything I could and had to face the fact that I needed to write that bloody review. *"Returning from the abyss that nearly swallowed him whole,"* I began, already frowning at my own hyperbole, *"Marc Gatton proved he's not out for the count just yet."* I carried on in this vein for another couple of hundred words, particularly proud of the section about Marc being *'lithe as a mountain goat'.* I'd once had a bet with Zoe about just how ridiculous I could make my features without anyone remarking on it and the habit had never left me. Sometimes, it's the little things that get you through the day. And Marc was definitely more of a goat than a fox—to my current state of mind, at least. I'd just got to *'Black Swans might just be on the comeback trail—assuming their leader finally makes good on his promises to stay clean, if not always sensible,'* when Tris came banging through the door and flounced onto my desk.

"Well thanks for nothing, love," he sulked. "I wouldn't mind being a receptionist if I didn't have to talk to people." His face lit up. "But now you're here and you can tell me all about last night and that will cheer me up immensely." He bounced excitedly, making my desk shake.

"Calm down, Tigger," I said, rescuing the pens that were about to fall onto the floor. "And I'm sorry to disappoint you, but there isn't much to tell. Although I did have a run in with one of the writers from the Gossip, so I'm half expecting there to be a made-up story in that this week." I sighed.

"Who cares?" said Tris. "You're the one with the rock star boyfriend, they can go suck it. Or did you do that already?"

I laughed, despite myself. "No, I did not," I said, crossing my fingers under the desk. "Honestly Tris, it was a fun night but there's nothing much going on with me and Marc. He shot off early this morning for god knows where and I have no idea if or when I'll even see him again." Tris looked disappointed and was clearly gearing up to dig for more, but was interrupted by Arthur sticking his head out from his office.

"Nice of you to join us, Jem," he said mildly. And then to Tris, more sharply, "don't you have photocopying to do? Oh, and I've had someone on the phone demanding to know why

I don't care about cats—that wouldn't be anything to do with you, would it?"

Tris groaned and stood up. "Laters, Jem." He slunk off towards reception and Arthur fixed his gaze on me instead.

"Can I have a word?" he said, immediately turning back into his office. Ugh. He'd better not be planning to give me shit about coming in late. It was a running joke with the rest of the staff that I was rarely away from the office. It wasn't that I loved the job itself—I was happy enough with it, but it was far from the perfect media career my teenage self had imagined whilst daydreaming about the future. The real reason I was so dedicated to the Mercury was that I just didn't have much to do with my spare time. Dan was always working late and I didn't feel like going out on my own. It was far easier to work all day, every day and just convince myself that the early nights were good for me. I owned the flat outright, thanks to mum being fully paid up on her life insurance when she had the nerve to go and die on me, so Dan had moved in for comfort rather than financial support. If he wasn't actually in the flat, no one would even guess he lived there—he hadn't wanted to put any pictures up or shift things around when he moved in, even though I suggested it as a way of making him feel more at home. Apart from some clothes tucked neatly away inside the wardrobe and a rack of vinyl albums that he geeked out about with his mates occasionally, there was no sign of him. I could have gone out on the town with Zoe, of course. She still invited me to glitzy events with determined regularity, even though she knew that the answer would almost always be no. Zoe had always been more of a party animal than me and never took offence when I turned her down, so I'd found it easy to gradually slip into suburban domesticity. On the odd occasion that I did go out with her, I secretly hoped that it might re-ignite some kind of passion in Dan if he heard tales of soap stars chatting me up, or reality show 'stars' telling me how fake it all was before throwing up in the bathroom of a soulless hotel whilst I looked on supportively. But nope—nothing seemed to bother him. He got up, went to work, came home, watched football on television and seemed utterly confident in my adoration of him without feeling the need to make any real effort. Zoe often said she couldn't understand what I saw in him. Sometimes—just sometimes, usually when I was sitting home alone for the fourth night in one week—I wondered the same. Still pondering life and love and whether I really should sort out my social life, I wandered into Arthur's office and sat in the chair opposite his desk. He had a serious expression on his face as he turned to me.

"I'm assuming there'll be a good article out of the last few days' activities?" he asked. A twinkle lurked in the corner of his eyes, which was a relief. "What's going on with this chap then? Do me and your dad need to go and have words with him?"

I tried not to snort at the idea of two well-meaning old men asking Marc Gatton if his intentions were honourable. "As I keep telling everyone," I said firmly, "there is nothing going on between us. We got on well and he invited me to the awards thing because his friend's wife was going on her own. He was just playing to the cameras."

Arthur looked unconvinced. "He seemed quite keen, from what I could see. Anyway," he brightened, "it's a bit of a scoop for the little old Mercury, isn't it? Having our reporter get up close and personal when all the others were basically told to piss off, from what I hear." *Not personal enough to worry about walking out on me this morning*, I thought uncharitably. "How are we going to make the most of this then, Jem?" he asked.

I frowned at him in confusion. "I'm not sure what you mean?" I said, genuinely confused. "The Black Swans piece will be in by this afternoon, as promised. I'm not sure what else you want me to do with it?"

Arthur gave me what I assumed he thought was a conspiratorial wink. It made him look like a slightly deranged stoat. "Ahem, well," he cleared his throat, "I've got a friend at one of the big dailies who rang me when he realised that it was one of my girls out with Gatton." I bristled at the 'girls' comment, but kept my mouth shut, waiting for what I knew was coming next. Arthur at least had the decency to blush as he blurted it out. "How about telling him your story? You know what they want—the usual, 'my night with,' etcetera etcetera. If there's nothing going on then you might as well make something from it. It's not as though you're going to bump into Gatton out here, is it? They'll pay good money. As well as, erm, a cut for The Mercury, of course." *A cut for yourself, you mean*, I thought as I stood up, trying very hard not to cry. One of the things I really hated about myself was my tendency to cry too easily. It made me look like a complete drip, when actually it was more often caused by frustrated fury. I'd had many embarrassing incidents with shop managers and traffic wardens over the years.

I took a deep breath and looked Arthur in the eye. "You should know better," I said quietly, "than to try to sell your staff to the highest bidder. God only know what my father would say if he got wind of your behaviour." Arthur shrank a bit at that. He was very fond of declaring himself an old fashioned gentleman. "I'm fairly sure it would mean the end of

drinks up at the golf club, at the very least. Now, if you don't
mind," I said, standing up, "I've got work to do. I'm going to
pretend that we never had this conversation, Arthur. Because
if it really happened, that would make you nothing more than a
grubby old man who'd sell his principles to the highest bidder."
The embarrassed silence told me everything. Arthur wasn't
really cut out to be a cutthroat media whizz and he knew it. I
stalked out of his office, careful to close the door rather than
banging it behind me. My anger levels had gone way past door-
slamming and into pure, cold fury. Steph turned to speak as I
walked through the office, but thought better of it when she
saw the expression on my face. I sat back down at my desk
and stared at the piles of work I really ought to be doing. That
bloody Black bloody Swans piece could go, for a start. I gave it
one last spellcheck and pinged the submission button before
I could change my mind. I got through the rest of the day in
silence, headphones wedged tightly in my ears and my furious
typing just daring anyone to attempt to speak to me. Even
Tris didn't bother me—an unheard of miracle. I checked my
diary and found an interview I'd forgotten to schedule in the
excitement of my week so far, so I made arrangements to do
it in town the next morning. If nothing else, it would keep me
out of the range of office gossip.

Having grumbled all the way home and up to the flat, I
scrabbled for the light switch in the dark and dumped my bags
onto the kitchen table. I wondered briefly why the curtains
were already drawn, before remembering that I hadn't been
home for the last two nights. Two nights—was that really all
it had been? The Sunday newspapers were still piled up, half-
read, on the sofa. Life had still been completely normal at the

weekend, with only the lurking anxiety about Marc's interview preventing me from concentrating on the Sunday supplements. It still was only the middle of the week, but it felt as though a bomb had been dropped into the centre of my world and the ripples were still travelling outwards. It occurred to me that the closed curtains meant that Dan presumably hadn't been home either. I checked my phone. Fourteen texts and four missed calls. Shit, what if there'd been an emergency and I hadn't picked up? My initial panic faded as I scrolled past the oldest ones, which seemed to consist of nothing more than updates on how much he'd had to drink, how much Joe had lost at poker and why he wasn't home yet. The last message had arrived only half an hour earlier.

Hey babe, where are you? Stayed at Joe's last night, had a late one in town.

Just as I was trying to think of something bland to say, the phone rang in my hand and I nearly dropped it in surprise. I banged the accept button before I could change my mind.

"Hi babe!" Dan was clearly struggling over background noise. "That big American deal came through and the boss gave us the rest of the day off to celebrate." I remembered Dan talking about a deal he was working on, but I hadn't got a clue what it was actually about. In fact I wasn't entirely sure I even knew exactly what Dan's job involved, besides money and suits and a lot of shouting. "I'm in the Uppy with the lads", the Uppy being the local name for the Uppingwood Arms, "why don't you join us when you're finished hobnobbing with the stars?" Someone laughed behind him.

It was the last thing I wanted to do, but I couldn't think of an excuse that wouldn't sound weird. "I'm at home," I said, gazing around the bedroom. If a stranger had been asked to guess at who lived in the flat based only on its contents, they'd assume it belonged to a single woman. Dan really did keep everything shut away from the rest of the world. "I'll just have a shower, then pop over."

"Cool, babe!" The phone went dead and I sat staring at it, wondering what I was going to do. I'd slept with another man, for christ's sake—I didn't have any choice but to come clean. Or at least, to break things off with Dan in as nice a way as possible; I'd rather not bring Marc into it, especially after the previous twenty-four hours' weirdness. But what I now knew with absolute certainty was that I wanted more from life—even if making the leap was even scarier than I'd ever imagined. I started the shower running and got undressed whilst waiting for the boiler to clank into life. Inheritance might have paid for the flat itself, but it didn't cover maintenance—I was going to have to suck it up and call the servicing company out sooner rather than later. I thought briefly of Arthur's earlier suggestion and all the problems it would solve. The amount of money a tabloid would pay would be enough to fix pretty much everything that needed fixing. *No.* Regardless of Marc's behaviour, there'd be a price for selling my story and it wouldn't be financial. I'd never be able to look myself in the eye if I did something like that. I resigned myself to taking on as much extra work as possible over the next couple of months, as I tipped my overnight bag out onto the bed in the hope of finding my phone charger. Finally unraveling it from a tangle of musty clothes, I felt something sharp tucked inside a stale-looking sock. Wriggling my hand inside to investigate, I discovered the card that Marc had left on the bed. I turned it over in my hand, wondering whether I should dare to just call him and ask him straight why he'd been so weird with me this morning. No, that would be desperate. And however mixed up I was feeling right now, I wasn't desperate. Well, not yet, at least. Sighing, I tucked the card underneath the music box Mum had given me as a birthday present when I was tiny. "From me to you," she'd said, and I'd kept it in pride of place in my bedroom ever since. I wasn't trying to hide the card, I told myself, I was just keeping it safe. But who from, I wasn't entirely sure.

I could hear Dan before I'd even got through the door of the pub. He was in the corner by the fireplace with Will and Stevo. If anyone else was sitting at that table when they arrived, the three of them would position themselves as close as possible and glare balefully at the interlopers until they moved. They'd been friends since school and it showed. Their conversation was often incomprehensible, littered with nicknames and references that they thought made them sound cool but actually betrayed their grammar school upbringing.

Dan stood up as I came in, waving his half-finished pint at me. "Get the drinks in then, Jem," he called. "We're waiting to hear all about what you got up to with Gatton last night." My stomach lurched as Stevo guffawed loudly.

"You been hobnobbing, Jem?" I gave him a weak smile and headed to the bar, Stevo's voice following me. "You put on a good show of being a groupie, lass," general laughter, "our Dan needs to watch out, I reckon." Grimacing to myself, I made my way to the bar past a family trying to persuade their shouty toddler to eat his chicken nuggets instead of throwing them onto the floor. The pub was quieter than usual and I found Gina, the Uppy's longest-serving barmaid, perched on a stool behind the counter with her face buried in a magazine. She looked up with interest as I approached.

"Ooh Jem," she said, putting the magazine down in a puddle of beer. "I saw you on the telly last night! Looked proper posh, it did." She rested her elbows companionably on the bar top and grinned. "You leaving Dan for a pop star, then?"

I sighed. "Sorry to disappoint you, Gina, but I'm pretty sure Marc Gatton does that to lots of people." She didn't look convinced. "It was work," I insisted, "I had to go along with it. I'll have a gin and tonic and whatever those three are drinking." Gina wasn't going to be put off that easily.

"It didn't look like work from where I was sitting," she said as she put my drink in front of me and started pulling pints for the boys. "If I was you," she leaned across and dropped her voice, "I'd be sticking to Marc Gatton like a fly to shit." She took my money and winked as she passed over my change. I muttered my thanks and headed over to the corner with the tray of drinks. No one offered to help. Dan grinned at me as I wedged the tray onto the table and passed him his pint.

"Cheers love," he said. "Here's to you and your television debut."

Will spoke for the first time. "I'd have been so pissed off if that had been my Sarah on the telly," he informed me. "It's a good job Dan isn't the jealous type." Dan leaned back in his chair and I noticed that the light coming in through the window shone off the thinning patch at the back of his head.

"Jem's not the unfaithful type, are you love?" said Dan, not bothering to wait for an answer. "She knows when she's got it good enough. Who'd want to get up to anything with that filthy has-been, anyway?"

"He's a nice bloke," I muttered, "there's no need to be mean." Dan raised an eyebrow and I backtracked. "He knows how to put on a show."

"Yeah, we saw," said Will. "Anyway, it's not like he'd be interested in anyone like you, is it?"

"You insulting my missus?" Dan bristled. The only thing worse than other people fancying your girlfriend was other people not fancying your girlfriend. It was like sitting with schoolboys. Or cavemen. *Me Dan, you missus.* I took a gulp of my drink—might as well keep my alcohol levels topped up.

Will ploughed on. "Nah I didn't mean that," he said. "Jem's all right, like," *well thanks for that vote of confidence, Will,* "but she's not the groupie type, is she? Good steady girl, aren't you Jem?" He looked at me as if he'd paid me a genuine compliment.

Stevo had gone outside to smoke and returned smelling of stale tobacco. He picked up his pint with a grunt. "Cheers Jem. You're not running off with that Gatton bloke then?" He looked round at the table. "What?"

"We've already covered that," I said. *"Apparently,"* I glared at Will, "he wouldn't want me even if I was up for it. So you can all stop worrying."

"Oh we weren't worried," said Stevo in a kindly tone, "it's not the sort of thing you'd do anyway, we all know that. When are you and our Dan going to make it official, anyway?" I felt myself blush.

"I'll get round to asking her one day," said Dan as I stared at the floor. "No rush, is there Jem? Those eggs of yours have got a few years before they dry up completely."

For fuck's *actual* sake. I drained my glass and put it on the table. Standing up, I patted my pockets to make sure I had my phone and house keys, then turned to Dan, fixing what I hoped was a realistic smile onto my face. "I'm knackered, I need to get an early night. No, it's fine," he'd moved to get up, "you stay here and have another. I'll be asleep before you get in." Dan looked relieved and sat back down. I could hear them ordering more beer before I'd even made it out of the door.

ESCAPE TO HIGHGATE

It was already daylight when the alarm went off painfully close to my head. Dan had staggered in after closing time absolutely hammered, but had somehow made it up and out for the office again without waking me up. The only reminder that he'd even been in the bed was a faint scent of Eau Sauvage and hairspray on the pillow next to me. The alarm was still shrieking and I scrabbled for my phone to hit the snooze button, but it didn't stop. Staring blearily at it through a curtain of tangled hair, I realised it was actually a call from an unknown number. And apparently it was already nine o'clock. I must have fallen asleep before setting an alarm the night before. I tried not to panic as I picked up the call. In my experience, unknown numbers generally meant that something awful had happened.

"Hello? Is that Jem? *Will you shut up?*" a vaguely familiar woman's voice shrieked over the sound of children yelling in the background. "Not you," she said hurriedly, "just bloody kids determined to see me into an early grave. *FUCKING SHUT UPPP!*" The voice was now unmistakably that of Suzie Fisher and, judging by the clattering noises in my ear, she had apparently just dropped her phone into a bucket. I propped myself up and waited.

"Hello?" she said again. "Are you there or am I talking to thin air?"

"I'm here," I grinned at the phone. "Overslept. Erm, how are you?"

There was a groan at the other end. "Don't ask. I bloody love my kids and one day you will see us together and I won't be shouting at them. But today is not that day. Fuck's *sake*. Hang on a minute." I heard muffled cursing and thuds at the other end and then she came back on the line sounding much clearer, if a bit echoey. "I've locked myself in the bathroom," she said. "It's the only place I get any peace some days and even then one of them will start banging the door if I dare take too long having a piss. Anyway, I managed to get hold of you, yay! Lovely Tristan on your reception desk knew who I was and gave me your number. You mustn't shout at him, okay?"

"Of course I won't," I said, lying through my teeth. "It's nice to hear from you. Sorry I left without saying goodbye, I was in a bit of a rush."

"A rush to leave because Marc was being a weird prick, you mean?" She carried on before I could say anything. "Look, I know it must seem strange, but he isn't really like that these days and I refuse to let him mess this up. You're the first person I've known him with who I can bear to be around and I'm not giving up that easily." I didn't know whether to be flattered, or just morbidly curious about Marc's usual standards in women. I switched the phone to loudspeaker and got out of bed. I needed to get dressed if I had a hope of getting any work done this morning.

"How do you know he was being, erm..." I floundered, before deciding that honestly was almost certainly the best policy with Suzie, "...a weird prick?" I managed to find some reasonably clean jeans in the laundry pile and wriggled into them as I spoke.

She laughed. "Because I've been friends with him for years and know him almost as well as I know Paul," she said. "And, well, he had a bit of an emergency yesterday morning and really didn't have any option but to disappear. It wasn't anything you did. Look," she said, as I sat on the edge of the bed pulling on a sock, "Mum's coming over to look after the kids today *thank fuck* and I need to go into town to get my nails done, because I am sick of looking like I live in a skip. Can we grab a drink at lunchtime? Kings Cross?" Fate clearly had plans for me, so who was I to fight them? And it would be nice to see Suzie.

"I'm actually due at a meeting at that end of town this morning," *or at least I will be if I can get my act together*, I thought, dragging the other sock on and wondering whether the laundry pile actually ate all my decent bras, "I could meet you afterwards?"

"Perfect," she said, and I could already hear banging in the background. Clearly the kids had realised where she was. "One o'clock at the Lincoln Lounge on York Way. Drinks are on me. *FOR CHRIST'S SAKE!*" She rang off abruptly, leaving me wondering why I'd ever thought that having kids might be a good idea.

Despite the fact that I was running late and rush hour was pretty much over, the tube was still packed. I found myself wedged into the armpit of a sweaty businessman who frowned at me as though he was worried I might be getting a thrill out of it. Did people get turned on by sweaty armpits? I guessed some must do. It would have to be attached to a nicer looking body though, I decided, and managed to twist myself away as someone got off at a stop. Big mistake. My backside was now pressed up against him and that definitely wasn't just his wallet I could feel through my jeans. I wondered if it was accidental, but as he pressed himself harder against me, I realised he was absolutely aware of what he was doing. Ugh. I managed to wriggle my arm free and, pretending to reach down for something, brought my elbow back sharply into his groin. He cursed and a couple of people turned to look.

I smiled brightly at him. "Oh, I'm sorry," I said, raising my voice so that people could hear me clearly, "did I hurt you? Maybe next time you'll think twice before pushing your pathetic cock against women's arses." He went puce, standing rigid and speechless as people around us muttered disapprovingly. With perfect timing, we came to my stop. I gave him a shove for good measure as I pushed my way out of the carriage.

"You go, girl," yelled a middle-aged woman still on the train and I grinned at her as it pulled away. The puce pervert was still onboard, trying desperately to pretend nothing had happened. I had quite a spring in my step by the time I finally made it to my meeting—especially as it was with someone I already knew. Larger than life and jollier than Santa after Christmas, everyone thought that Jonty Beckett had lost his mind when he announced he was leaving Uppingwood to run a microbrewery in Kings Cross. But he'd proven the doom-mongers wrong, carving a niche for himself amongst drinkers who wanted something better than a chain pub but definitely didn't want to have to crowd in with hipsters and pay four times the going rate for the privilege. The Old Tavern was tucked down a side street that had hardly any passing foot traffic, but the pub itself was always busy. I'd been to its opening night and again with Zoe a couple of times since, but this was the first time I'd seen it empty. A tiny girl with cropped black hair that made her look like an elf was wiping down the tables.

She stopped and looked at me as I walked through the front door. "Hey, you must be Jem?" Elf-girl was Australian. Zoe had a habit of picking up other people's accents—'wandering accent syndrome', I called it—and went through a phase of constantly using questioning intonation after briefly working with an Australian intern at the Gossip. She'd only stopped when Tris took to asking her if she'd put a shrimp on the barbie whenever he saw her. I was pretty sure that I'd never heard an actual Australian ever mention either shrimps or barbies. This particular one came bouncing over and I wondered how anyone managed to be that chirpy first thing in the morning. "I'm Crystal," she said. Well, at least it wasn't Kylie. "Jonty's out back cleaning the lines, he says to send you straight through." She led me down past the bar, with its endless rows of gin and whisky. Jonty didn't believe in many spirits other than gin or whisky. Crystal pushed open a heavy door at the back of the bar and ushered me through into a covered yard, where I could see the top of Jonty's head poking out from behind a rack of barrels.

He straightened up as he heard us. "Hey Jem! Thanks, Crystal love, we'll be back through in a minute. Put the kettle on?" She disappeared back into the bar. Jonty clambered out from behind the barrels and hugged me warmly. "Lovely to see you, Jem," he said. "How's your dad? Jill still keeping him on the straight and narrow?" I laughed. Dad was possibly the straightest man I knew. If anything, it was Jill who'd calmed down since they got together.

"Yeah, she's just about got him under control," I said. "How funny is this?" I gestured around us. "Me coming to interview you about life in the big bad city."

Jonty grinned. "I bloody love it, Jem," he said. "Upping-wood's lovely, I grant you, but you'd think it was a village out in the sticks sometimes, not a mainline suburb. It's those middle class hippies that keep it like that, all grow your own chickens and the like." I wasn't sure that Sid and Nancy would appreciate being described as middle class (although they undoubtedly were), but Jonty was right about Uppingwood itself. There was definitely a 'hipster village green' air about it that suited the kind of people who earned sky-high wages designing office blocks from artisan desks in bare white loft conversions. Nancy herself was some kind of interior designer, although you'd never know it to look at her. I only believed it myself because I'd once witnessed her leaving the house in a spectacular Vampire's Wife dress complete with matching skyscraper heels on her way to a design award ceremony that was being held, she'd informed me, on a repurposed warship temporarily moored on the Thames. She'd explained what the awards were about whilst I was emptying the tub of vegetable peelings into the bin and I hadn't been listening, so it had been a surprise when I'd peered out of the window later that evening and spotted her tottering her way into the back of a cab. I strongly suspected that Sid was more militant in his attitude and probably didn't get invited to the parties alongside her. Or maybe Nancy just didn't want to take him.

"This is a real pub," Jonty continued. "We get all sorts in here—city boys, youngsters, locals—and they like it because it's *proper*. I'm looking for a manager, you know, if you're at a loose end?" he eyeballed me and I pretended I hadn't heard him. "I've got backers interested in helping me take on another place over in Barnes, this place is going to need looking after in my absence."

I rolled my eyes at him. "I've already got a job, Jonty," I said, "and a place like this is a bit bloody different from doing occasional shifts at the Uppy." And I hadn't even done that since I was in my teens.

Jonty looked unperturbed. "You'd be great," he insisted, "and we need to get you out of that suburban rut you're in. Come on, let's have a cuppa while we talk." He headed back in through the doors. "Bloody good coffee is the other thing," he said as he fired up the machine behind the bar. "You have it black, yes?" I nodded. "Good girl," he said approvingly, passing me a utilitarian white mug brimming with the black gold, "don't bother spoiling it with any other muck." He tried not to wince as I rooted around in my bag for a little plastic box and promptly dropped a sweetener into my drink. I compounded my offences by stirring it with a ballpoint pen that I found in my pocket. "Anyway," he said, through faintly gritted teeth, "how are you in general, love? Been up to much?"

"No," I lied, "quiet as always. Jill's got dad redoing the back garden and Arthur's as grumpy as ever." Jonty laughed. They were all in a similar age bracket, which in Uppingwood meant they automatically knew each other. People of Jonty's age still talked of others as 'incomers' if they'd moved to Uppingwood in the last twenty years. Sometimes I wondered if there was an invisible bubble over the town that kept it separated from the outside world.

"Yes," he continued, "but how are *you* getting on, Jem? Last I heard, your Dan was moving in. You planning marriage and babies yet?"

I sighed. "Come on Jonty, I'm here to talk about you," I protested. "Let's get cracking on the story of how you moved to the big city and made your fortune, eh?" This was the sort of thing I could churn out every day without even thinking about it. Self-made success stories loved talking about themselves and the Mercury's readers loved hearing about it. They'd either be envious of Jonty's success, or they'd enjoy thinking about what an idiot he was for leaving staid and comfortable Uppingwood in favour of the grubby city that most of them had escaped years ago. The lunchtime service was well underway by the time we were done and he was too distracted to remember his plans to quiz me on my love life, so I gave him a quick hug and made my escape before he could get nosey again. He shouted after me as I was disappearing through the crowd.

"Think on that job offer, eh?" he said. "You're wasting away out there." I shook my head in disbelief and headed out onto the street.

I didn't know the bar that Suzie had suggested meeting at and was surprised to find that it was even more tucked away than the Tavern. I'd expected her to favour glitzy cocktail bars, but this was, well—'down to earth' was probably the best I could come up with. A gaggle of intimidating-looking bikers sat smoking outside and for a minute I thought I'd got the wrong place. But no—there was Suzie, bouncing and waving at me through the window. As I approached, the nearest man pushed himself off the wall and lurched forwards. I stopped in my tracks, but he merely turned and opened the door for me.

"Takes me ages to stand up straight with my back," he grinned. "I'm getting old." He mock-bowed and ushered me in.

I needed to spend more time in the city, I decided—living in Uppingwood was making me insular and suspicious. I did have occasional moments of bravery, as with the pervert on the tube, but too often I made the suburban mistake of automatically thinking the worst of people. Just because a city was busy didn't make it full of arseholes. Okay, so there was going to be more idiots—but you're also way less likely to bump into them. Most people, I reminded myself, were basically decent.

"Hey, hey!" Suzie practically squeaked as she jumped up to hug me. She was wearing a wrap dress and knee boots with huge sunglasses perched on her head and looked every inch the rock star wife. I wondered for a second what the hell I was doing. People like me didn't have friends like Suzie, we had friends like, well… Actually, when I stopped to think about it, most people would put Zoe into the same bracket as Suzie. I suppose it had just never occurred to me to think about the 'cool girl' schtick because I'd known Zoe forever. "Let's have cocktails," Suzie said. " I don't get out as often as you might think." She walked over to the bar with me and grinned up at the barman, who was clearly already under her spell. "Today calls for mojitos all round," she declared.

"I'll have a gin and tonic, actually," I interrupted. "Lots of tonic." The barman nodded and walked off.

Suzie tilted her head to look at me. "I do like people who know their own mind," she said and turned to look around the pub. "Believe it or not, I really don't go out very often. I've got a few friends from years back—school and the like—but we have such different lives these days that it's difficult to keep up with each other. They always think I'm going to be too busy having fun to see them. "It *is* fun, don't get me wrong," she took her drink from the barman with a grateful smile and slurped it greedily as she waved her bank card at the payment machine, "but I'm still me, you know? I didn't turn into a different person the day I married Paul." We took our drinks over to the table and sat opposite each other. "I'm sorry," Suzie said, "I'm over-sharing again, aren't I?" She pulled a face.

"No," I reassured her, "I'm just finding it hard to believe that you don't have a million people hanging around wanting you to go out and have fun with them."

"I could go out every night if I wanted to," she sighed. "There are plenty of people who'd like to be seen out socialising with Paul Fisher's wife, even after all these years. And that's the problem, isn't it?" She sucked on her straw. "I'm the gateway to the band. Excitement, the rock and roll lifestyle, all that crap. I have a good life, don't get me wrong," she grinned. "The kids are surprisingly adorable when they're not trying to kill each other, my mother loves Paul possibly more than she loves me and therefore helps out all the time and, well, the money obviously helps." She picked a mint leaf out of her glass and bit it with tiny sharp white teeth. "Mmm. Yes, money helps. Whatever anyone says to the contrary, it really can buy happiness. But it can be really fucking boring, all the same."

"Tell me more about the other wives and girlfriends," I said. "Aren't they in the same boat as you?"

Suzie laughed. "Are you *kidding* me?" she snorted. "Oh my god, I have honestly never met such a bunch of fuck ups in my entire *life*. Although I quite liked Marc's ex. You know about Rachel?" She squinted at me and I shook my head. I knew he'd been married and that it had been over years ago, but gory details had been thin on the ground—and I'd definitely looked for them. "It hasn't really been in the press—they lost interest in him when he didn't die. Rachel got into drugs at the same time. She was just trying to keep up with him really and he's always blamed himself for it. Anyway, they had a daughter." She saw the look on my face. "Yeah, Alice. No one knows about her apart from close friends and family. Mostly because Rachel was a full-blown addict by that point and social services were going to take the baby away as soon as she was born." She crunched down on an ice cube with an expression of deep satisfaction. "Marc's mum, Heather, took Alice in," she continued. "Moved to the countryside and brought the baby up pretty much on her own, but Marc visits a lot. His dad left when he was still a kid, so now it's just him, Heather and Alice. Rachel visits occasionally, but spends most of her time in France. Off her head in the Parisian suburbs, bless her."

I sat silently absorbing the information dump for a moment. "How old is Alice now?" I asked eventually.

Suzie sipped her drink again before answering. "God, I love mojitos," she said, running her tongue along her lips, "however naff they might be. Anyway, Alice will be seven this summer. I'm her godmother. Fuck knows what the poor kid did to deserve that." A snort. "I see her quite often, actually. And Heather's great. Much younger than her age, if you know what I mean. You'd need to be if you were suddenly landed with a baby to look after just as you were planning your retirement. Every now and then Marc tries to get her some help with the childcare stuff, but Heather always refuses. Says she doesn't like people interfering. And Alice is a gorgeous little dot, not an ounce of trouble."

"Does Marc see much of her?" I asked.

Suzie nodded. "Yeah, he and Alice adore each other," she said. "He'd like to have her living with him full time, but it's just not possible. He can play the doting dad all he likes, but he'd never stop the music and that means being away a lot. Heather gives her the stability she needs. He visits a lot, though. In fact," she looked up at me through her long lashes, a serious expression on her face, "that's where he disappeared off to yesterday morning. Rachel's reappeared, for the first time in ages. And she only appears when she's in trouble." A deep sigh. "I practically had to beat the information out of Paul, but I gather she's pissed off the wrong dealers this time—done a runner and made the mistake of heading back to England. She usually sees Alice at one of those mediation places, but somehow she found out where Heather lives and turned up on the doorstep, screaming that she wanted her daughter back. Alice was terrified, of course. All she's ever been told is that mummy's poorly and lives in a different country most of the time—she didn't have a clue what was going on. Heather called the police and Rachel's currently being held somewhere. Probably for psychiatric assessment, if previous incidents are anything to go by. So when Marc got a call from his mum first thing yesterday morning, he just raced off to the rescue without really thinking about anything else."

"Where is he now?" I asked.

"Still at his mum's," said Suzie, stirring her drink with a freshly manicured fingernail, purple glitter polish sparkling against the ice cubes. "Daddy makes everything better, as far as Alice is concerned. I'll go visit her when things have settled a bit. Marc will only be able to stay with her a few days anyway—the band's due to fly to America next week." I felt my heart sink. "They're not away for long," she said, seeing my expression. "Couple of big venue gigs, just to make sure everyone knows they're back. Next year will be the busy one—Mike's got plans for a world tour. I reckon he's milking the cash cow while he can, because both Marc and Paul have been thinking about ending their contract with him and he knows it. There's a break clause coming up."

"Break clause?"

"Yeah," she replied, "a sort of 'get out of jail free' card they have the option to use every few years. They've been with Mike since the beginning—nearly thirty years, now. Time flies when you're having fun," Suzie waved at the barman and gestured for new drinks, "or when you're so off your head that you lose track of time and you're not awake long enough to ever realise that your management's taking you for a ride. The minute Marc got his faculties back, Mike knew his time was up. Wendy will never get over it." She snorted loudly. My phone pinged and I flipped it over to read the message. It was from Dan.

'Headed out early, no rest for the wicked! Try not to shag any pop stars today :D'

"Boyfriend?" asked Suzie in a sympathetic voice.

I looked up. "How did you guess?"

"Because you rolled your eyes and sighed as you read it," she grinned, "and I've seen enough Boring Boyfriend Syndrome in my time to recognise the signs." I grimaced as she sucked on her straw, an impish smile on her face.

"What am I going to do?" I asked. "Dan thinks I love him!"

Suzie looked thoughtful. "You could always be truthful," she said, "and tell him you've dumped him for the man of your teenage dreams? Thank yoooou," this to the barman, as he took our empty glasses and replaced them with fresh ones. I took a large gulp of my gin and tonic and wondered if it would help to get blind drunk rather than going home and sorting things out with Dan. Suzie tilted her head as she gazed at me. "I'm only half joking, you know." I looked up, unconvinced. "You like Marc, right?" I nodded mutely. "And he likes you." I wished I could have her strength of conviction after his behaviour the last time I saw him, but didn't say anything. "Come *on*, Jem," she spoke more sharply, "what the fuck are you doing with an office monkey who's already middle-aged? Because you don't seem the type to settle down to a life of happy homemaking in the 'burbs, quite frankly." She sipped her drink and leant backwards against the seat, appraising me coolly. "Do you need this bloke of yours to help you pay the bills?" I shook my head. "Lucky you," she said. "But are you happy?" I looked up, confused. "I mean, *actually* happy," Suzie continued, eyeing me beadily as she spoke. "What are your plans with this chap of yours—do you even *want* a future with him? Marriage and babies and years of domestic bliss until one of you finally loses their shit and finishes the other one off with the salad servers before burying them under the patio?" She laughed, but I was surprised at the sudden feeling of sick fear in my stomach. That *was* the plan, wasn't it? Well, apart from the bit about murder. Move in together, have a tasteful wedding (service at Uppingwood church, reception at the Uppy, because that's where all Uppingwood weddings had their reception), probably push out a baby in a couple of years time. Suddenly it wasn't sounding so attractive. And when I thought about it, Dan and I had never actually discussed any plans. I mean, that's what I *assumed* would happen, but perhaps he didn't want to? Or maybe it was me who didn't really want to. I wasn't sure I knew *what* I wanted anymore. I stared gloomily into my drink until Suzie leant across the table and put her hand over mine.

"You're, what? Thirty?" I nodded. "I'm forty-five next month," she saw my surprise, "I know, I don't look it. And before you ask, no I haven't had any work done. My theory is that I look halfway decent because I stopped giving a fuck years ago. You have to, in this business. I stopped caring what people thought about me and stopped caring that I didn't have a career of my own. I don't *want* a career, is the god's honest truth of the matter," she grinned, "I'm quite busy enough keeping on top of life and making sure my kids don't go entirely off the rails as they grow up. That's why I bring them with us to events. It might not be the normal life that most kids have, but it's better than being shut out in the country and never seeing their dad, whilst living with a mum who's permanently off her face on booze and meds. Don't get me wrong," she twirled her straw thoughtfully, "I can totally imagine myself in that situation—if I was on my own with the kids all the time I would *want* to be off my face. But I love them dearly and the best I can do is to try to keep us all functioning as a family." She looked me straight in the eye. "Marc's a good man, Jem. And you're a good woman. You'd suit each other. I know, it's easy to get carried away sometimes—god knows, I've done it plenty. Look," she rolled her eyes and took a deep gulp of her drink, "you're clearly not happy at home or you wouldn't have thought about doing anything at all. When's the last time you had sex with someone on a job?" I pulled a face, "Exactly. And it doesn't matter that you already had a crush on Marc—aah you're blushing!—you wouldn't have done anything if you weren't at least subconsciously looking for an escape route. I can't tell you whether things could work long-term between you and the delightful Mr G, but I'd really like to think they might. He's an old romantic under the surface. He needs some stability, you need a reason to cut loose and have some fun. You're good for each other." I sat staring into my glass, wondering—not for the first time this week—how the hell I'd got into this ridiculous situation. Just as I was debating whether I should have another drink in order to calm my anxiety, Suzie sat upright.

"Look," she said, gathering her things together, "why don't you come home with me for the day? You can keep me company whilst the kids try to give me a nervous breakdown and then Paul should be home later—we could go out and have some fun. Please?" She batted her eyelashes. I thought about it for a minute, wondering whether it would be too much to leave Dan home alone for a third night. Then I remembered the conversations in the Uppy about how reliable and steady I was, and how Dan often didn't come home at night without ever worrying about what I'd think. Maybe it was time to start kicking those apple-carts.

"Yes," I said, thinking that Arthur wouldn't dare argue with me having a day off right now, "that sounds like fun."

WONDERLAND

Suzie and Paul lived in a very beautiful Georgian house in Highgate that was set behind high automatic gates. She tapped a code into the entry box and a smaller entrance to the side of the gateposts clicked open.

"It's not much, but it's home," she said, grinning. It really wasn't a massive house by Highgate standards, but was set back on a tiny side street that was an oasis of greenery in comparison to the traffic-rattling Archway Road behind us. There were only a few other houses on the street, all of them undoubtedly worth millions. Suzie ignored the ornate front door with its pillars and giant potted olive trees and headed down a path to the side of the house instead. I could hear shouting as we went past the windows, before a door opened ahead of us and a small brown-haired boy tumbled out. He ran to Suzie, who scooped him up.

"She's stolen Mr Bean *again*," he wailed. There were no tears, just righteous indignation. "She *knows* it's my turn to play with him today!" Suzie chuckled and turned to speak to me over her shoulder.

"This is Teddy," she nodded down at the boy, "and Mr Bean is the cat. Who has the sense to stay out of the way as much as possible." As if hearing his cue, a fat tabby shot out of the door and disappeared at high speed down the garden. The furthest side of the garden was immaculate. There was a patio with lounge chairs and umbrellas set out next to a built-in hot tub—a definite upgrade from the cheaper inflatable versions that were ten-a-penny in the back gardens of Uppingwood. Carefully tended flowerbeds were set amongst perfect green grass. The area closest to us, however, looked like a bombsite. It was dominated by a large wooden climbing frame, with a swing that had been spun right over so many times that it now hung only a few inches below the top rail. There was a seesaw next to it, with soggy-looking teddy bears balanced on the seats. The climbing frame itself sat in a sea of mud and I could see a single forlorn glove being slowly swallowed up by the earth. There was also a distinct trail of muddy footprints between the garden and the house. This was definitely a family home, possibly of the feral variety.

Teddy suddenly seemed to register my existence. His head shot up and a pair of chocolate brown eyes surveyed me intently. "Who are you?" he demanded.

"This is Jem," his mum told him. "Be nice."

"You're Uncle Marc's lady," he announced. "I heard Mummy talking about you to Daddy. They like you."

Suzie laughed and put him down so that he could lead the way into the house. "Yes we do," she said, "which is why we are all going to behave whilst Jem is in the house. Okay?"

"What sort of gem are you?" asked Teddy, ignoring her. "Some gems are better than others."

"Jemimah is the very special kind," said Suzie. "Now go tell grandma we're home for the day—she can escape if she likes." Teddy ran off into the next room and I heard his bare feet hammering up through the house. Suzie put the kettle on. "Thankfully the cleaner came yesterday, so I'm not as embarrassed about the state of the place as I'd usually be."

"The state of it?" I snorted, speaking for the first time since we'd arrived. "It's practically palatial and I'm pretty sure that you know it." I peeked through the door that Teddy had disappeared through and saw a huge living space with an open fireplace and a giant fake bearskin rug on the floor. The glamorous image was only spoiled slightly by the potty that was lying on its side next to the armchair.

"I'll give you the grand tour in a bit," Suzie said with a grin. "I do love it here. It's peaceful, but close enough to everything that I don't feel too lonely when Paul's away." Teddy came flying back into the room, followed by a smiling, dark-haired woman who I assumed must be Suzie's mother. She was carrying a gloriously cute small girl who had her thumb in her mouth and a concerned look on her face.

"She was trying to stick a bow to Mr Bean's head," the woman laughed, "but he didn't take kindly to having a clip in his fur. He doesn't like it, does he Maude?" The little girl shook her head and then looked at me.

"Who dat?" I grinned at her.

"Hello Maude," I said, "I'm Jem. I'm very pleased to meet you." Maude nodded but said nothing. Her grandmother, however, lit up.

"Aah so you're the one they've all been talking about," she exclaimed, shifting Maude to her other hip so that she could shake hands. "I thought you looked familiar. I'm Maureen, always known as Mo. It's so lovely to meet you finally. Suzie's told me a lot about you."

"Suzie seems to have been talking to a lot of people," I said drily, "considering that she's only known me a couple of days."

Suzie grinned unapologetically. "Like I said, it's not often I like anyone that Marc's associated with since the divorce." She held her arms out to her mother, who passed Maude over to her. "So I make the most of it when I do. Although come to think about it," her face scrunched into a frown, "it's never actually happened before." She turned to her mum. "Are you heading home for a bit?"

Mo nodded. "Might as well make the place look like someone's home occasionally," she said. "It's a miracle I haven't been burgled."

Suzie sighed. "You know it's bound to happen at some point," she said, and then turned to me. "We've been trying to get mum to move in here for at least the past year, but she refuses. Refuses our hospitality! Don't you, you ungrateful old bat?" She grinned at Mo, who made a pretence of slapping her.

"What I did to deserve you, I do not know," Mo sighed, rolling her eyes. "She's nicer than people think," this was to me, "but she hates showing weakness. Don't you, pumpkin?"

Suzie rolled her eyes. "Shut up with the pumpkin crap," she snorted. "People might start to suspect I'm nicer than I let them think." She poked her mother with a sharp talon. "I mean it about living here though. You know I do. It just makes sense. And you could help with the kids more." She pasted a sad puppy expression on her face.

Mo laughed at that. "If I helped out any more with these kids, people would start assuming they were mine, not yours. Talking of which, I'm assuming you want me back tonight? As Jem's here?"

Suzie ramped up the pathetic expression. "Oh *please*," she said, "if you could bear it? Paul might be back though, if you'd rather not."

"Paul doesn't get enough time off," said Mo, firmly. "If he comes back in time he can go have fun with you girls, can't he? It would do you good to have your husband around a bit more, Suzette." Suzie caught my raised eyebrows.

"Yeah, my name really is Suzette," she sighed. "For god's sake don't tell anyone though. Mum's the only one who gets away with it these days." Mo grinned as she picked up a bag from underneath a side table and zipped her jacket.

"She's my crepe suzette, you see," she explained to me with a grin, "sweet but makes you feel sick if you have too much of it. See you later!" She ducked back out of the kitchen door before Suzie could throw the teapot.

"This is the playroom." Suzie was giving me the promised tour. We were currently picking our way over discarded toys in a room almost as big as my entire flat. She saw my expression. "Yeah it's big," she said, "but we figured the space might as well be used. If the kids weren't in this bit it would just be some overdressed dining room with a huge table that no one ever sat at. That's certainly what it looked like when we bought it. Poor old place was unloved and mostly empty."

"How long have you lived here?"

"Couple of years, now." Suzie picked up an oversized stuffed toy rabbit and threw it into the corner where it joined a pile of other stuffed toys in what looked like a furry orgy. "We lived out by my mum, but then the band started picking up again and Paul was away so much that I started feeling isolated. It's nice having babies out in the countryside, but when you're a town girl at heart it doesn't take long before you're bored and start getting into trouble."

"I thought your mum just said she lived in town?"

Suzie was on her knees, picking up crayons. "Fucksake, don't kids put *anything* away? Yeah, mum used to live with my gran near St Albans. But then Granny died and mum could see I was losing my shit up there, so she said she'd move down as well if I could persuade Paul. Gran's house went for enough money that it bought mum a little studio place over in Hornsey and left enough for her to live on. And Paul does okay out of royalties." She straightened up. "Marc's always insisted on things being split evenly between the band, despite it being mostly him and Paul. Kieran and Stef don't really have much input, but the boys insist that Black Swans wouldn't exist without them, so everyone gets the same." She looked idly at a lurid pink hair scrunchie, before throwing it into the toy pile. "And it's a *lot* of money," she said with a grin. "Enough to keep me in the lifestyle to which I have become accustomed, for one thing. And Paul does pretty well out of it—we love each other enough to not ask too many questions when we're apart for a long time, and things work out okay for everyone. The kids have a stable home life and I'm not going quietly batshit alone in the country." I'd picked up the scrunchie and was twisting it round my fingers.

"So you're telling me that in order to keep a relationship going, you both see other people?"

Suzie patted my arm. "Sweetie," she said in a kind voice, "it works for us. Chances are it wouldn't work for you—but then, I don't think it would work for Marc, either. He's the monogamous type." She pulled a face. "When he's not being a dick, that is. Anyway," she said, "let me show you the rest of the house."

By the time Suzie had finished showing me around, I was

starting to think that I could probably learn to cope with this kind of life. The house was expensively old and beautifully preserved, with tasteful furniture and bedrooms that were vast but somehow still cosy. By the time she showed me her walk-in wardrobe I had full on envy, and said so.

"The funny thing is," she said, closing the door on the rows of clothes rails, "I usually just wear jeans and a tshirt, whatever I'm doing. Mostly this stuff stays hanging on the rails. But," she wagged a finger at me sternly, "don't ever let anyone tell you that having a stupid amount of money isn't an advantage in life. Of course it bloody well is. No one really believes that the road to true contentment lies in not being able to pay the gas bill, do they?" She flopped down onto the king-sized bed, which was made up with crisp white bedding. For some reason I'd half expected satin and leopard print.

"You'll stay over tonight?" she asked hopefully, from her prone position on the bed. "There's a spare room that hasn't been used in way too long." It was certainly tempting, especially as the alternative was to go home and deal with the boyfriend I'd betrayed. Running away from the problem wasn't remotely classy of me, but right now I had no idea what I was doing. And I definitely needed time to think.

"That would be lovely," I said. "And if I can talk things through with Marc at some point," I went on, "maybe we can at least be friends."

Suzie looked downright sceptical at that. "You're telling me you want to just be friends with him?" She snorted. "I saw how you two looked at each other, Jem. The entire bloody world saw it! Get a grip, love. He'll either sort his personal shit out or he won't, but if he doesn't then he's an idiot." She clearly had more to say, but suddenly there was the sound of doors opening downstairs and kids shrieking in excitement. "Daddy's home," she grinned, pushing herself upright and clambering off the bed. "Come tell Uncle Paul all your problems whilst I find us some nice, medicinal gin."

Paul was attempting to offload his bags onto the kitchen table with a child hanging from his neck and another clinging to his legs. He turned and grinned as we walked in, his brown eyes twinkling at the sight of us.

"Did you kidnap her?" he asked Suzie. "Shall we have a drink to celebrate?"

"On it." Suzie was already pulling glasses out of a cupboard with one hand and waving a blue glass bottle in the other. She banged doors open and I heard ice clinking. Paul scooped Teddy off the worktop and shooed him out of the room. "Go put the telly on for your sister, mate," he said. Teddy shot off and kids' television almost immediately began blaring from the other room. Paul clicked the door shut on them.

"Paul will tell you the same as me, Jem," she said, kissing her husband's ear and making him grin, "Marc's been miserable for years and now he isn't—or at least, he wasn't—and the difference is already huge. Also, parties are much more fun now I've got company. Talking of which," she peeled herself off Paul and waved the gin bottle in the air, "let's go out and have some fun."

"Come dance with me!" Suzie waggled her glass in my face and staggered slightly, giggling as she put a hand out to steady herself on a man sitting at the next table. He looked quite happy to be used as a perch as she swung off him, blonde hair flying and cleavage pressing up against his back. His girlfriend sitting opposite was another matter entirely and I pulled Suzie away before she accidentally started trouble. The bar was heaving. It was the sort of place I'd normally avoid like the plague—although I doubted that in normal times I'd have even been allowed past its hallowed entrance. Tucked down a side alley that led off an expensively quiet Mayfair street, it didn't even have the usual velvet ropes in front of the door to cordon off the queues. Instead, it was set behind a small roofed courtyard with a discreet security guard opening the door for those deemed suitable. My heart had sunk as we approached—I'd spent too many evenings blushing with embarrassment behind Zoe whilst she argued her case for admittance with just such doormen. She usually lost, and I once asked her why she even bothered. Surely it would be easier to just go to places that would let anyone in?

"If they let just anyone in then I don't want to go there," she'd retorted. I didn't bother pointing out that we always ended up in those places anyway. But, this time, the door had been opened with nothing more than a polite 'good evening' and a casual gesture ushering us inside. With black woodwork and blood red walls, the bar reminded me of some of the dingier clubs I'd been to in my youth. The carpet here definitely wasn't sticky, though. It was far noisier than I'd expected after the quiet of the street outside—this part of town clearly expected its residents to fit proper soundproofing to avoid annoying their oligarch neighbours. Paul had immediately been stopped by a dark haired man who I recognised as the lead singer of a band who were definitely on the up—at least, according to Zoe and her office gossip. He was chatting away enthusiastically as Paul made the internationally recognised sign for 'get me a drink' over his head.

"You'll love it here," Suzie announced confidently, having to shout into my ear to be heard. "No one gives a shit who you are and they serve decent cocktails." She stopped to shriek at a tall black woman in a red silk dress who I vaguely recognised from a late night arts programme. The woman fought her way over to us and hugged Suzie tight.

"I haven't seen you in months, you ignorant bitch," the woman said.

Suzie laughed. "I've been busy earth-mothering, haven't I? Have to earn my keep occasionally." She turned the woman round to face me. "Talia, this is Jem. Jem, Talia is one of us. She can be trusted with *anything*."

Talia snorted as she shook my hand. "I've had to learn to be, with Suzie around," she said. "I'm not sure my liver has quite recovered from the last time we went out. And my reputation certainly hasn't. Anyway," she extricated herself from Suzie's grasp, "I need to be off, I've got a live recording tonight. Why don't you both come sit in the audience sometime soon?" She smiled at me. "You can watch me being professional and then we'll go out and prove to the world that I'm really not."

"I'd like that," I said.

"Then it's a date." Talia hugged Suzie, gave me a little wave and disappeared back into the crowd. No sooner had she disappeared, than I was suddenly grabbed from behind in a shrieking bear hug.

"Oh my god Jemimah you have *escaped!*" Tris screeched in my ear, turning me round but not letting go. "And would you just *look* at yourself, girl?" I could see myself in the mirrors on the back wall, so did as I was told and looked at my reflection. I definitely had more makeup on than usual, but that was down to Suzie taking over before I'd been allowed to leave the house. She'd also dressed me as if I was an oversized doll, ignoring my grumblings as she threw clothes at me from the depths of her capacious wardrobe.

"It's an excuse to get some wear out of them," she'd said. "And whilst I *obviously* think you're completely marvellous, darling, I really do have some standards on a night out." So I'd been forced out of jeans and tshirt and into a slinky satin dress that looked more suitable for the bedroom than a public outing. I'd got my own back by insisting on wearing my ratty leather jacket over the top, which Suzie had begrudgingly decided was, "definitely a strong look". None of this explained why Tris was currently hanging off my neck whilst staring at Suzie in the manner of an abandoned puppy trying to woo a potential rescuer.

"Ooh, Jem's new best friend!" he squawked.

Suzie laughed. "And you must be Tris," she said over the noise, holding her hand out. He dropped me like a hot stone and actually caught her hand and kissed it, the arse-licking slime ball. I'd get revenge for this. I didn't know how, but it would happen. I settled for treading hard on his foot.

"Oh I'm sorry Tris," I said, "I didn't realise you were there,"

He narrowed his eyes at me. "What are you doing here anyway?" he asked. "It's not like you to be in town all gussied up like a Christmas tree."

I glared at him. "If you could stop looking so bloody surprised when I'm dressed even half decently, that would be nice. Anyway," I pointed out, "it's not like you to be in this neck of the woods. Looking for upmarket trade?"

Tris pulled a mock-horrified face. "Ooh you bitch!" he shrieked. "You're not far wrong though," he waved at someone over my head and I turned to follow his gaze. "Over here, Simon!" he called, beckoning through the crowd. "Turns out that Simon's sister used to date the owner, so I've been able to get in for the first time ever. In fact," Tris turned to Suzie, "I'm pretty sure this is also the first time Jem's been anywhere like this," he ignored me pinching his arm, "because it's all a bit upmarket for that dull boyfriend of hers." He grinned at me brightly and I had never been so close to punching him in the face.

Suzie rescued me. "It's very lovely to meet you, Tristan," she said, "but we're on a flying visit. We'll catch up with you later, okay?" With that, she pulled me away towards the bar before he could utter another word.

"Let's get a quick drink whilst Paul finishes his dullsville conversation," she said, "then we'll go through."

I was confused. "Go through where?" I looked around the tiny room and couldn't see anywhere she could mean. And Tris was already dragging Simon through the crowds toward us. Suzie ignored me in favour of elbowing her way to the bar and putting in her order. Somehow she never had to wait to be served—I definitely needed to pick up some tips on that one. Presenting me with a very large glass, she winked. "Follow me," she instructed and headed off towards the sign for the toilets. Bemused, I trailed behind her. Just before the Ladies was a door bearing a sign declaring it to be a cleaning cupboard. Suzie knocked it in what sounded distinctly like a set pattern and—like something out of a spy novel—the door creaked open. She tugged my arm. "Come on," she said, stepping inside.

"Shouldn't we wait for Paul?" I asked. I looked round but he was nowhere to be seen.

"He'll find us," Suzie cackled, and stepped into the darkness.

An hour later, I had just about managed to get the astonished expression off my face. The room behind the door had turned out to be another bar, but this one was exclusive enough to give Zoe wet knickers for a week. I was reasonably certain that Tris wasn't going to turn up in here to embarrass me. In accordance with Suzie's prediction, Paul had indeed appeared just after us. I'd tried to buy a round of drinks, only for Suzie to tell me to put my purse away.

"It's a tab system," she explained. "We pay the bill automatically."

"You come here a lot then?"

She grinned. "Not nearly enough for my liking, but Paul's away a lot and doesn't like me coming here alone."

"I don't like you doing what now?" Paul appeared at her shoulder.

"You don't like me having fun," Suzie pouted and he laughed.

"You have enough fun for all of us," he said. "If you had any more fun you'd collapse through exhaustion." She stuck her tongue out at him.

He turned to me. "Enjoying yourself, Jem?" he asked. I nodded. "Marc used to like it here," he continued. "Maybe he'll start coming back now we've lured you in."

I frowned. "Right now I'm not sure Marc wants to be lured *anywhere*."

Paul looked unfazed. "Aah get on with you," he said, sounding more confident than I felt, "he won't leave you alone for long. After all," he turned to put his empty glass on the table, "you're one of us now."

HERE COMES TROUBLE

T*his is actually fun*, I thought to myself as I was spun around the dance floor by an actor who I vaguely recognised as a minor character from a major television series. I'd barely sat down since we walked into the club, only taking a break from dancing when I needed a refill. Even Suzie had given up by now and was currently sitting on Paul's lap in a booth by the tiny dance floor, cheering me on.

"Can I see you again?" my partner yelled hopefully in my ear. I stopped dancing and pulled back to look at him properly. He was tall, with floppy hair, a nice smile and muscles I could feel through his expensive shirt. Cute, if you liked that sort of thing. I just laughed in response and pulled him back onto the dance floor, a confused look on his face. I was definitely getting increasingly wobbly on my feet. I swung round to my patient partner with the intention of kissing him on the cheek, but to his evident delight I stumbled and accidentally caught him smack on the lips.

"Sorry," I yelled at him, nightclubs not being ideal for small talk. Unfortunately he didn't hear what I said and decided to take full advantage of my apparent change of heart. Pulling me towards him, he was clearly aiming for full tongue contact. I was trying to wriggle away when someone came up behind me and knocked him flying into the crowd. Trying to balance on the ridiculous stilettos that Suzie had insisted on me wearing, I spun around to find Marc standing in front of me with a look of absolute fury on his face. And—oh, just fucking brilliant—Angie was hopping around behind him, trying to pull him back. Before I could say anything, he grabbed my arm and stalked off, forcing me to stagger after him. Suzie belatedly registered what was happening and ran after us as Paul picked my unfortunate would-be suitor up off the floor. I could see him brushing the poor man down and offering to buy him a drink as Marc dragged me towards an exit, pushing Angie away as she made another vain attempt to stop him. I was shouting at him to let me go but he didn't listen, just hauled me with him out of a side door and onto the street. A couple who had the misfortune to be walking past as he banged the door open almost fell over in shock and stood staring at us as they realised who it was that had sent them flying. But before anyone had a chance to say anything, Suzie shot out of the door behind us and smacked Marc round the back of his head with her bag. It brought him up short but he didn't let me go.

Ignoring our rapidly expanding audience, she rounded on him sharply. "What the fuck are you playing at?" she demanded. "Manhandling women now?" I noticed out of the corner of my eye that one of the burly doormen was hovering beside us at a careful distance. Other drinkers outside the club were being less discreet and a couple were filming. Oh well, it would give the Gossip some more column fodder.

"I'm fine," I reassured her, but fury was building up inside me and it was going to have to come out somewhere. I finally managed to drag my arm out of Marc's grip and turned to face him. "How fucking *dare* you?" I hissed. He just stared at me tight-lipped, unfathomable emotions racing across his face. "I was having *fun*, Marc!" I wailed. Behind him, I could see Angie walking towards us. She was looking nervous.

"Isn't Jem *allowed* to have fun, Marc?" Suzie spat. Angie came up beside her and Suzie turned to look at her. "And what are *you* doing here?" she demanded, "are you on protection detail again?"

"Leave her alone, Suzie," Marc snapped, finally breaking his silence. "It's not what you think. Angie," he looked at her, "go home, okay? I'll ring you tomorrow." Angie looked as though she wanted to punch every last one of us in the face, but with a final snarling grunt, she turned and stalked off down the street.

"So what *is* it, Marc?" I asked. "You're allowed to do what you want and disappear whenever you like, but I have to ask permission to go anywhere? That's fucking bullshit and you know it." I was close to him now, the pair of us bristling like cats about to fight, each debating whether to make the first move.

"You can do what you like," he finally said, quietly enough that I had to step even closer in order to hear him, "always. But I really wish it was me you wanted to do it with."

I was sure I'd misheard him. "Do what with you?" I asked, feeling as though I was somehow teetering on the brink of a precipice. If I fell now, I might never escape. Marc held my gaze and I felt my stomach instinctively curl with need and desire.

"Everything," he said.

I considered this for a moment before replying.

"Make me."

Marc moved so quickly that I didn't see it coming. Before I realised what was happening, he'd slung me over his shoulder and was striding off down the street, as I shrieked with laughter and tried not to drop my bag. I owed Suzie a pair of shoes already—one of them had fallen off as Marc picked me up and the second disappeared into the gutter, as he swung round to leave.

"You kids have fun, now!" Suzie called after us as we staggered down the street away from her. I craned my neck up from my position halfway down Marc's back and saw her sitting on the pavement, doubled up with laughter. Paul had walked up behind her and was just staring after us in amazement.

"Put me down!" I squealed, still laughing. Marc ignored me and just kept walking, one hand gripping my backside to hold me in place and the other stuffed in his pocket. He looked—from an upside down perspective, at least—for all the world like someone casually walking home with their bag over their shoulder. It was just that in this case, the bag was a ten stone woman who was definitely going to puke if she wasn't upright again very soon.

"We're here now, anyway," he said, turning down a back street and stopping suddenly in front of a large and ornate back door set into what looked like a blank brick wall. Unearthing a card key out of his pocket without letting go of me, he opened the door onto a thickly carpeted hallway with huge gilt-framed paintings along the wall. A muffled squeak of surprise from ahead of us made me peer round, still hanging down Marc's back. There was a reception desk at the end of the hallway, staffed by a woman in teetering heels and a fitted black dress who had come out from behind her screen to see what was

137

going on. I thought she might have wavy red hair, but I was concentrating on not falling onto the floor by that point. Not that Marc seemed inclined to let me go.

"Evening, Maddie," he said brightly, "you know what it's like when you don't fancy walking home in your heels."

I peered round at the upside down woman and gave her a wave. "Nice to meet you," I said weakly. Maddie arched an eyebrow, but was too well mannered to say anything. She stepped backwards and pressed the button for a lift that was set into the wall at the end of the hallway. Marc stepped inside and turned carefully, so that I didn't bang my head on the walls of the tiny cramped space.

"Thank you, Maddie," he said. "Excellent service as always." The doors closed just as Maddie finally collapsed into laughter.

"*Shit!*" I landed on the enormous bed with a bouncing thump. I had just enough time to register that we were in the classiest hotel room I had ever seen in my life, before Marc was stalking his way up the bed on his hands and knees. When he was right over me, he stopped and gazed down.

"You still have clothes on," he observed. The motion sickness had subsided now and I stared up at his glittering grey eyes in the dim light. God, but he was beautiful.

"You are so delicious, Jemimah Holliday," he said, bending to kiss me. "Now let's get some of these things off you." As I was already barefoot and wearing nothing more than knickers and Suzie's tiny dress, it didn't take long. "That's better," he said finally, a satisfied grin creasing his face, "now I can say hello properly." As his head slid down my body, I nearly panicked at the prospect of such unexpected intimacy. Marc must have felt me trembling, because he slid his hands back up to grab

138

mine and raised his head to look at me. "All of you," he said quietly. "I want *all* of you." I groaned as he found his target and let myself give in to sensation.

I woke up just as dawn was breaking through a crack in the curtain to feel Marc pressing up against me from behind. He was hard as a rock and had his arms wrapped around me as he wriggled into position.

"Is this okay?" I mumbled assent. "Hang on," he said and pulled away from me slightly. I kept my eyes shut and didn't move as I listened to him rustling around in what I assumed was a bedside drawer. There was the now-familiar sound of foil ripping and some fumbling going on under the sheets, before he slid back up against me. "Safety first, as they say," he murmured, nipping my neck with sharp teeth and making me gasp. "Aah," he sighed, finally sliding inside me, "fucking hell, you feel good." I said nothing, just pushed back against him in time with his slow rhythm. He slid one hand down and felt for me in just the right place to make me start moaning quietly as he pushed deeper inside me, his movements quickening along with his desire. His free hand grabbed my hair and pulled my head back so that he could bend into me and nip my neck as he thrust harder, forcing me ever closer to the brink. Just when I thought I couldn't bear anymore, he gave up all pretence of gentleness and forced me over onto my stomach, fucking me so hard that I thought I might howl with the sheer animalistic joy of it. I crashed into my own release just as Marc gave his final gasping thrust, crying out as he collapsed on top of me. We stayed like that for a while, both struggling to catch our breath. I felt the weight of him on top of me, as if he wanted to melt right down into my bones. Finally, he shifted onto his elbows and lifted himself up slightly. I opened one eye and peered awkwardly round at him, unable to stop myself grinning as I did so.

"Funny, am I?" he asked, raising an eyebrow. He thrust into me and even though he was subsiding by now, it made me gasp. "That's better," he said, bending to kiss my cheek. "Why don't I run you a bath?" I groaned as I felt him finally slide out of me, but couldn't find the energy to move.

"*Owwww!*" he'd fetched me a sharp slap across my backside and I scrambled round to face him. He stood at the end of the bed, stark naked and grinning.

"I couldn't resist," he said, shrugging. It was difficult to keep my eyes on his face, but I did my best. "I'll run the bath. This one's big enough for two."

"When are you going to tell your boyfriend?" Marc asked, as he soaped my back. He'd been right about the bath being big enough for two—a giant claw-footed monster, I was pretty sure you could fit a five-a-side football team into it without too much of a squeeze. I was sitting between his legs in front of him and he'd occasionally slide a hand round to soap my front. I leaned back against him and sighed.

"Today, I guess," I said. "There's no point putting it off anymore. Even if we weren't doing…this," I twisted my head around to kiss him briefly on the mouth, before settling back against him again, "it's obviously over. It should have been over a long time ago." Marc gave me a squeeze, sending water sloshing over the sides of the bath onto the black and white geometric tiles of the bathroom floor.

"Do you regret meeting me?" he asked, his arms tightening slightly as he spoke.

I gave a short laugh. "How could I regret any of," I waved my arms vaguely in the air, "this?" I took hold of one of his hands and held it in mine underneath the water, gazing at the contorted view of our entwined fingers. "I don't want to be a kept woman," I went on, "but I'd like to have a partner in crime." I twisted to look at him. He was smiling down at me, his damp hair plastered back against his head. I wished I had a time machine, just for a split second, so that I could go back and tell Teenage Me just what a strange twist her life would take. At precisely the moment I thought I'd got it all worked out, Marc Gatton had appeared and turned my entire world upside down. "I'm sad about hurting Dan," I said, "but I'm not sad about breaking up with him. He deserves someone better."

I could feel Marc frowning without even looking at him. "Better than you?" he asked. "Don't you think you're good enough for a city boy?"

"Better for *him*," I replied. "Dan isn't a city boy really, he just likes to think he is. But he has a steady, well-paying job and nice enough friends and that's all he wants or needs. The trouble is," I idly stroking Marc's thigh and wondering how difficult it would be to have sex in a bath tub, "I've realised that I want more than that. From life," I wriggled round to face him, "from work, and from any man I might end up with." His appreciation of my soaking wet nakedness was evident even through the bubbles and I slid a hand down to grasp him as he closed his eyes and slumped his head backwards against the tiles. I later discovered that the hotel sent the bill for the replacement flooring to the Black Swans' accountant, labeled 'structural damage due to unacceptable guest activity'.

DIRTY STICKY (CAR) FLOORS

"**I**'d better find you some clothes," Marc said, after we'd finally emerged from the bath and curled up together for a while to dry off. He climbed off the bed and walking over to a heavy oak chest of drawers that was set against the opposite wall. There was a coffee machine on top of it and he switched it on. "Want one?" he asked, waggling a cup at me. It was made slightly disconcerting by the fact that he was starkly and unapologetically naked.

"Yes please," I said, wrapping a towel around myself and sitting up in order to make the most of the view. His wiry frame was taut and—considering he was nearly twenty years older than me—annoyingly short on saggy bits.

He turned round with my coffee and caught me staring. "Does Madame like what she sees?" he grinned, dipping into a very inelegant curtsey and making me laugh.

"Very much so," I admitted. "Although I guess we really should get dressed at some point today."

Marc put the coffee down on the table next to me, bending to kiss me as he did so. "I'm going to take you out for lunch," he said, sliding under the sheets next to me. "But first," a devilish grin, "I'm going to have you as my starter."

142

When we finally managed to drag ourselves out of bed, Marc informed me that we were heading out of town.

"I've got a car here," he said, watching as I wriggled into the same faded Black Sabbath t-shirt he'd been wearing the first time we'd properly met. It was too tight over my chest, but was at least clean. I was already wearing a pair of his jeans—ancient and faded and soft with wear—over boxer shorts that were definitely tighter on me than they would have been on their owner. "What size are your feet?" he asked, eyeing my bare toes wriggling in the deep pile of the rug that lay on the floor next to the bed. Before I could reply, he'd gone to the wardrobe and came back holding a pair of Adidas sneakers. "They're too small for me, I hardly ever wear them," he said. I peered in at the label to discover that they were only half a size bigger than I usually wore, and pulled them on. I picked my jacket up off the floor and slung it over my shoulders, catching my reflection in the bedroom mirror as I did so.

"I look like a reject from the 1980s," I remarked, twisting round to see myself from different angles. Marc came up behind me and put his hands on my shoulders. We looked at each other in our reflections.

He looked thoughtful for a moment, and then grinned. "I *am* a reject from the 1980s," he laughed, sitting on the edge of the bed in order to pull on a pair of battered black snakeskin boots. "What's your excuse?"

I watched him for a minute, thinking about how his personal history was so much longer than mine. "What's the story with your ex?" I blurted out before I could stop myself. Marc leaned back onto his elbows amongst the crumpled remains of what had been crisp white bedding and held my gaze.

"She's the mother of my child," he said, slowly, "and for that alone, she deserves my support, if not my respect." He eyed me speculatively. "We both did things we're not proud of, Jem," he said, "and we lost each other along the way. But," he pushed himself back upright and sat on the edge of the bed, still watching me, "I decided that I would claw myself back for Alice's sake. Rachel," he looked away briefly, "hasn't got to that stage quite yet."

"Where is she now?" I asked.

Marc smiled thinly. "With friends in Brighton," he said. "They've promised to make sure she stays there until I can sort things out. It's not ideal," he sighed, "but there isn't much else I can do. I can't have Alice being scared half to death by her own mother, but neither am I going to bail Rachel out every time she fucks things up. It's a form of enabling—no really," he'd obviously caught my doubtful expression, "if she thinks she's got a safety net, she'll never have any incentive to sort herself out. And I do want Alice to have a relationship with her mother, even if I can't stand the woman. Mums are important."

"They are," I agreed, feeling unexpected tears pricking behind my eyes. I turned away and rummaged in my bag, so that Marc wouldn't see that I was upset. My phone was glowing with unread messages—I pressed the 'off' button firmly and tucked it out of sight.

I don't know what I'd been expecting a wealthy middle-aged musician to drive, but it certainly wasn't the small and very battered silver Nissan Micra that pulled up in front of the hotel's discreet front door where I stood waiting. The passenger door window opened—and stuck halfway down.

"Your carriage awaits, m'lady," he said with a grin, peering

144

out through the narrow opening. Shaking my head in disbelief, I climbed in and let Marc lean over to fasten my seatbelt as if I was a small child. "There's a knack to making it work," he said, as I'd stared wordlessly at him. As we pulled away into the traffic, I surveyed the car's well-worn interior. Three different air fresheners hung from the rearview mirror, but they didn't quite cover the aroma of stale food. The remains of a crumbled digestive biscuit lay on my seat and, peering down into the passenger footwell, I spotted the scattered remnants of a McDonalds Happy Meal lurking in the gloom. Well that at least explained the smell.

"Not that I'm disappointed or anything," I said, as we headed out of town, "but I kind of assumed that you'd drive something more flashy,"

He laughed. "Oh, I've got the flashy car," he replied. "This one's my mum's. It's easier in the traffic and apparently—according to her, anyway—my own car gives the impression that I must be lacking in the trouser department." He risked a sideways glance at me as the road widened and we picked up speed. "My mother is a zero-bullshit zone," he said, swinging into the middle lane without warning and forcing a large white Jaguar to brake sharply, its driver waving angrily through the windshield. "I'm heading back there later. I'll rescue my own car then, before my darling daughter decides to redecorate its interior with glitter pens. It's happened before," he said, pulling a mock-horrified face.

We'd been driving just over half an hour when Marc turned the car off the motorway and down a slip road that led immediately onto a country lane. It was sunny and he grinned as we sped along the narrow road—faster than was probably wise, considering that we were in what amounted to an oversized dodgem car. Just as I was about to suggest slowing down, Marc did just that, turning off through a wide gateway in front of a beautiful thatched pub. A huge and ornately lettered sign announced it to be the Cheshire Cat, a famed gastro pub that I'd vaguely heard of but never given much thought to, for the simple reason that it was very unlikely I'd ever actually visit. The pub was set well back off the road and Marc spun the little car in a swirl of gravel in order to park up under a large oak tree. As I climbed out of the Micra and brushed biscuit crumbs off my legs, a smartly dressed white woman in her fifties with eyes like a Siamese cat came out to greet us, her polite expression only just managing to mask the fact that she was clearly giving me the once over.

"Darling!" She greeted Marc with a hug and kissed him on both cheeks, before pushing him backwards so she could look at him properly. "We haven't seen you for such a long time! And this is?" She turned to look at me, her eyebrows raised. Marc laughed and put his arm round me, pulling me back against him. I resisted the urge to stick my tongue out and settled for smiling politely.

"Celine, meet Jem. Jem, this is my friend Celine." She and I nodded at each other, each immediately comfortable in the knowledge that we would never be friends. "Got a table for us?"

Celine nodded. "Of course. Always space for you, darling." I scowled at her back as we followed her into the pub, Marc ducking under the low doorway into what turned out to be a small and very cosy dining room.

"Don't be put off by Celine's pretensions", Marc whispered to me as she led us through to a booth at the back of the room, "she's lovely once you get to know her. And her husband's been a friend of mine for more years than I care to count." He spoke more loudly. "Is Charlie around today, Celine?" Celine pulled out our chairs and grabbed menus from the windowsill, passing one to each of us as we sat down.

"No, he's gone fishing," she said, with a roll of the eyes that told me that she didn't approve of fishing. "But he'll be expecting to catch up with you, now you're back," she warned.

Marc laughed. "I'd like nothing better. Perhaps the two of us," he gestured over to me, "could pop in on you both sometime." Celine raised an arched eyebrow and pretended she hadn't heard him.

"Shall I get you some drinks? Water for you, Marc?"

"Yes please," he said, "with ice and lemon. Jem can drink whatever she likes, of course. Gin and tonic?"

"I've had more than my fair share recently," I replied. Celine raised her eyebrows in a *'And don't we all know it'* kind of way, which I chose to ignore. "Soda and lime will be fine. Thank you." I smiled at Celine, who turned sharply on her heel, possibly to go find some rat poison to drop into my drink.

"So," said Marc, "here we are. And we have all our clothes on, for once." He grinned. "You're pretty when you blush, you know?" I was about to say something when I noticed two women at another table staring at us. Or, more accurately, at Marc. One was tapping on her phone—either googling to check it really was him, or updating her friends, I guessed. Marc saw me watching them and turned. They both blushed beetroot red at being caught out and turned their backs on us, but I could hear them giggling under their breath. A young woman dressed in the generic upmarket pub uniform of tight black tshirt and even tighter black jeans came over with our drinks. "Thank you," Marc said, as she put the glasses down on the table. "Could we order some food? I'm absolutely starving. I'll have steak—medium rare—with salad and broccoli, please. Ooh, and mushrooms. Jem?"

"That sounds nice" I said, "I'll have the same. But with the steak cooked blue, please. Thank you." The waitress nodded and disappeared. Marc was grinning at me.

"What? Have I got something in my teeth?" The way he was looking at me through those hooded green eyes made me wish he'd have me for lunch, rather than the steak.

He grinned. "I was just thinking about how refreshing it is, being around you," he said. "You don't seem easily impressed. It makes a nice change."

"Of course I'm impressed," I said, truthfully. "I'm impressed that I'm sitting here having a really good lunch when normally I'd be eating shop-bought sandwiches behind the reception desk with Tris. I'm impressed that at the beginning of last week I'd never met you, but now here we are. And I'm impressed that you seem to want to spend time with me, because," I took a deep breath and went for the honest approach, "I think you could probably invite pretty much anyone to have lunch with you and they would say yes." Marc's mouth twitched into a smile; and I guessed I was right—I couldn't imagine he was rejected very often. "So what I *am*," I said, "is confused. Because, when there must be endless better looking, better paid and better known people to be spending your time with," Marc sighed and put a hand across the table to take mine, "why are you sitting here with me?" We both sat there in silence for a few minutes, looking at our hands entwined on the table between us.

"I have no idea," he said, eventually. I raised an eyebrow, but he continued. "I have no idea, because I honestly can't understand why you're bothering with *me*. People expect me to live some exciting rock and roll lifestyle, but I've done all that already—and too much of it, by anyone's standards." He laughed and slowly pulled his hand away to run it through his hair. Staring out of the window, he continued. "I'm tired. Tired of being surrounded by people who are only out for what they can get and tired of having to prove myself again and again for the media who are only really interested when I'm doing something dramatic and preferably dangerous. And most of all I'm tired of cutting myself off from people who might be good for me just because I'm scared. Scared of letting anyone get close in case it turns out that I'm not good enough for them." He looked me straight in the eye. "So that's why I'm with you, Jemimah Holliday. Because I don't know if I'm good enough for you, but I think we might just be good for each other." We stared silently at each other for a long minute. I was the first to break.

"Doesn't that sort of thing get boring?" I asked, changing the subject. I nodded towards the women at the neighbouring table—they were eating now, but it hadn't stopped them regularly turning round to check what we were doing. "Not being able to go for lunch in peace, having people watching you all the time, being seen on television with a woman no one's ever heard of? That sort of thing?"

Marc had the grace to look embarrassed. "I'd like to say that I'm sorry about the television thing," he said eventually, "but I'd be lying. In for a penny, and all that." I concentrated on the bubbles in my glass, unsure what to say. Before I could think of anything to say, the waitress was back with our food. I tucked into my steak with glee, relieved that for once my request for almost raw had been heard.

"What?" I demanded. Marc was staring at me again. "You're going to give me a complex, if you carry on."

"I like the way you eat," he said, as I self-consciously picked a piece of steak from my teeth, "no messing about, just tearing into it."

I grinned. "Maybe you just bring out the animal in me." Our eyes caught and I felt Marc's leg press up against mine under the table. It was all I could do not to bite my lip in anticipation like the heroine of some trashy romantic novel. Christ, it was like I didn't even know myself any more. On the other hand, it felt good—very good—to be out with a proper adult. Dan had always given the impression that he was just playing at being a grown up and it was me who was ultimately responsible for making sure things got done. I was pretty sure I wouldn't ever have to play the maternal role with Marc.

I'd planned to refuse pudding, but Marc insisted on us sharing a bowl of profiteroles. He popped them into my mouth himself, much to the excited entertainment of the women on the other table, who had given up on subtlety and were now openly snapping photos. After a round of very good coffees, Marc called the waitress over and paid the bill, waving away my—admittedly token—attempts to split it, before suggesting we go for a walk in the grounds.

"Don't you want to say goodbye to Celine?"

"I'll see her soon enough," he said. "I come past here a lot—it's on the way to mum's house."

I couldn't resist the opportunity to do a bit of digging. "Was your daughter pleased to see you?"

His eyes immediately lit up. "She's always pleased to see me," he said. "Daddy's little girl, is Alice. I don't see her nearly often enough, but at least being with my mum gives her some stability. And she moved up to the local primary school this year. She's doing really well." A proud smile. His face crinkled up and his eyes sparkled. "Anyway, let's talk about you, Miss Holliday." He caught my hand and swung it, pulling me against him slightly.

"What do you want to know?" I asked. "I could go through my entire life history and it wouldn't take long. I'm not sorry about it—I've had my share of getting drunk and misbehaving," I saw the look on his face, "yes, even before I met you. I'm not a complete innocent just because I live out in the suburbs, you know. But I got it out of my system pretty much whilst I was still hanging out with Zoe, and then when she moved away and I saw her less, things naturally just settled down a bit."

Marc squeezed my hand. "I would never have described you as innocent, Jem," he said with a grin. "You've coped very well with being dropped in at the deep end, I'll give you that."

"Maybe," I replied, "but it's a strange life you all lead."

Marc frowned. "Not really," he said. "Not when you get used to it, anyway." We were walking on a path that ran down from the back of the pub along the edge of some open woodland. It was a glorious day—the sun was almost warm and there was a scent of lilac in the air. We walked in companionable silence, just listening to the birds and the distant sound of traffic.

Marc smiled up at the sun with his eyes half closed. "Don't you think traffic sometimes sounds like running water?' he said, which was sweet, if rather hopefully romantic. "Isn't this amazing? I actually feel happy right now." He turned to look at me. "It's not just the sun, either. I like being with you, Jem," He stepped down a slight bank into the woods and I hopped down after him. "Come here," he said and, before I realised what he was doing, he had me pinned up against a tree. He held my

151

hands up above my hand and leant his body against mind to hold me still. His face low close to mine, I could feel his breath on my cheek as he spoke. "You are the most amazing woman," he said. "And I want you more than I've wanted anyone in a very long time. I just can't get enough of you, Ms Holliday." His knee wedged hard between my legs and I felt myself shaking slightly in anticipation as he bent to kiss me. Letting go of my arms, he ran his hands up and under my tshirt as I clung to him and pulled him hard against my mouth. It was *definitely* time to let go and just see where things took me, I thought vaguely, as I clutched his hair and wished that jeans weren't quite so awkward to get off in public.

He broke away suddenly, looking back up the path. "We're about to have company," he laughed. I managed to pull my tshirt down just as the two women from the pub appeared round the corner. They tried to look surprised to see us, but I strongly suspected that we'd been followed. "Ladies," Marc mock-bowed as they passed and they could barely contain themselves, snorting with laughter before they'd even got out of hearing range.

I squinted after them. "Well that's given people something to think about," I said, rearranging my clothes in an attempt to not look like a complete trollop. Not that Marc's appearance was any better—his shirt was rucked halfway up his back where I'd been mauling him and his hair was sticking up in tufts all over the place. "Christ, will you stand still for a minute?" He stood obediently as I pulled his shirt straight and stroked his hair back into place, only the crinkle of his eyes giving away his amusement. I stood back to admire my handiwork. "You'll do," I declared.

"Want to come meet my family?" The unexpected offer

stopped me in my tracks. Marc was standing looking at me with a smile on his face as if this was all entirely normal. "I know it's a bit quick, but Mum saw you with me at the Saturns and I think she'd like a formal introduction."

"I, erm…well…"

His face fell slightly. "You don't have to if you don't want to," he said, the smile dropping, "I just thought it would be nice."

"Of course I'd love to," I stuttered, "I just, well, I'm surprised you'd want some random fling coming to meet your mother."

"Is that what we are?" he asked, catching hold of my hand again. "A random fling? Is that what you'd prefer?" I mumbled something that I hoped sounded negative but not desperate. "If you were just a…*fling*, I wouldn't have invited you out the other night," he pulled me against him, "and I most definitely," he bent to kiss me briefly, "wouldn't have declared my intent quite so publicly. So yes," he picked up my bag from where I'd dropped it and carefully hung it off my shoulder before putting his arm companionably around me and heading back towards the car, "I would like you to come meet my folks."

IN AT THE DEEP END

"*Daddy! You're back!*" The little blonde girl was squealing and running out of the house towards the car before we'd even stopped moving. Marc crouched down to catch her and scooped her up, twirling round so that her hair blew out behind her.

"How was school today, babycakes?" He put her down and she held his hand tightly.

"It was good! We had to clean out the guinea pigs and Henry pig must actually be a lady because he's had babies, but he's eaten some of them. Mrs Flint says we have to call him Henrietta from now on and she's taken the bits of dead babies out of the cage and cleaned it up. Oh!" She abruptly halted her very informative monologue as she noticed me standing on the other side of the car.

I smiled rather nervously and walked round to where they stood. "Hello," I said, holding my hand out. "I'm Jemimah. You must be Alice?"

The little girl shook my hand politely and looked up at me with a solemn expression. "Do you like guinea pigs?" she asked. "Because I think we might have some spare ones at school. If Henrietta doesn't eat them all."

Out of the corner of my eye I could see Marc trying not to laugh, but I managed to keep a straight face. "I do like guinea pigs, yes," I told her seriously. "I like dogs and cats as well. I like most animals, actually. I don't have any pets of my own though."

Alice's little face crumpled dramatically. "Oh that is *so* sad. Do you cry about it? Daddy," she said, not waiting for an answer, "I think you should buy 'mimah a pet. Maybe a kitten. Or a fish. You can pet some fish if they're big enough," she informed me with authority. "Anyhow, Nanny says you're to come in and show her your girlfriend." She turned back to me. "Are you my daddy's girlfriend?"

"Erm, well, I don't—"

"Yes, she is," said Marc firmly, and shooed Alice. "Lead the way, princess. Let's take Mimah to meet Nan." I hadn't been called Mimah since primary school, but I wasn't going to correct such a cutie. Or his daughter, for that matter.

"Hello love! We weren't expecting to have you back so soon, this is a treat!" I shouldn't have been surprised that Marc's mum didn't look like your usual granny. She was, after all, mother to a bona fide rock star and friends with Suzie Fisher. But it was still strange to see such a quietly glamorous woman come out of what I assumed was the kitchen door. Her house was small, cosy and old enough to make me think it was probably worth a fortune. A glance down the path that ran along the side of the house confirmed my suspicions—nothing but garden as far as the eye could see, which was an expensive lifestyle choice in these parts. "Ohhh, you must be Jem!" She reached out to hug me and, before I had time to gather my thoughts, I was wrapped in a fug of hair and Chanel No.5. "I'm Heather—Marc's mother, for all my many, many sins. Let me look at you," she pushed me back without letting go, "oh yes, I think we approve. It's about time this layabout sorted out his private life." She let go of me and playfully punched Marc's arm before hugging him tightly. "So lovely to see you again, darling," she said. "I thought you were staying in town tonight?"

"We were back in the area," said Marc, "having lunch at Celine's. So I thought it was as good a time as any to bring Jem over to meet you. My mother was very cross about the other night," he said, turning to me.

Heather rolled her eyes at him. "I wasn't cross, darling," she said, "I was just desperately hurt that you could have found this lovely lady and not brought her to see me before I discovered her existence via the dratted television."

Marc laughed. "Yes, well, it wasn't exactly planned." He draped an arm over my shoulders. "Jem was sitting there and I was in full dramatic flow, as it were, and, well," he squeezed me tight, "who could resist? The best bit of the story," he continued, as we followed Heather into the house, Alice having already gone skipping in ahead, "is that we met when she interviewed me. Luckily she gave me a good review." He winked at me and I blushed.

I decided it was about time I proved I actually had a voice in my head. "It's very lovely to meet you, Heather," I said, "Suzie's told me a lot about you."

"So you really are a friend of Suzie's?" Heather looked delighted. "Well that's that then, you must have truly been accepted into the fold. How are you feeling, Marc?" She frowned slightly and I saw a worried look on her face for the first time since we'd arrived. "I'm really not sure about you being back on the road you know, with all the temptations around." She turned to me again. "He's too easily led, you see," she said.

Marc just raised an eyebrow. He was clearly used to being talked about as if he wasn't there. "Mother likes to worry," he told me.

"With good reason," retorted Heather.

"Well there is that," he agreed and put an arm round her. "But I've managed nearly three years now, which is a personal record. And one I don't intend to mess up any time soon. Certainly not now that I've got much healthier distractions around, at least." He grinned at me. Heather looked unconvinced. "Look, Mum," he went on, "what else would I do with myself? I'm more likely to stay clean if I'm busy. And I can't live without the band, you know that. I only get into trouble if I'm bored."

"Has Mike got rid of that awful wife of his yet?" Heather asked, clearly deciding it was time to change the subject.

Marc's face tightened. "They suit each other," he said, levelly. "All Mike has to do is keep on top of the paperwork and he gets his twenty percent, so he's the perfect little nest egg for Wendy. And she likes to keep an eye on Angie, of course."

This was new information. "Angie?" I asked. "The one who clearly hates me? They're related?"

"I'll put the kettle on," said Heather and tactfully withdrew into the kitchen. I could hear her telling Alice to go get some flowers from the garden to put on the table as I rounded on Marc.

He sighed. "Angie is Wendy's daughter," he explained. "She started with us when she had to do work experience for college and Wendy thought that coming on tour for a week would be the ultimate case of one-upmanship. It turned out that she's actually really bloody good at her job, so we kept her on. She's seen me go through some pretty rough patches and gets a bit protective at times, that's all. She doesn't hate you." I thought Marc must be incredibly naive if he genuinely thought that, but didn't bother arguing. Just as he appeared about to continue, Heather bustled back in, carrying a tray laden with tea things.

"Let's have a cuppa," she said, sitting down and reaching for the pot, "and then I'll go find Marc's baby photos." She looked up and grinned at her son, who looked for all the world like a small child being embarrassed in front of his school friends. "Won't that be lovely?"

By the end of our visit, I knew that Marc had been a very cute baby (if a bit potato-like when lying naked on a picnic blanket) and that he'd been reasonably academic until the day he first picked up a guitar—a gift from Heather's parents, long since dead—and realised that being in a band got him far more attention from girls.

"And that was that," said Heather with a faintly rueful smile. "Not that I'd have him any other way, of course. Although I could have done without some of the more hair-raising moments." She caught Marc's expression. "Anyway, I'm sure you know enough about that already. More tea?" I also discovered that Marc hadn't been kidding when he'd admitted to usually driving something fancier than Heather's Micra. I'd already spotted a large garage alongside a patio that lay behind the house and, as we got ready to leave, Marc led me out to it. He pressed a button on his keys and the door rolled up to reveal the biggest, blackest car I had ever seen in my life. The last time I'd so much as glimpsed anything like it was when Prince William had been driven through Uppingwood on his way to open a local hospital.

"Bulletproof, I assume?" I asked drily.

Marc laughed. "I'm not that important," he replied, "thankfully. I just enjoy driving." He stepped forward and stroked the car's bonnet as if it was a favourite pet. "I'd always wanted a Bentley, but could never justify the cost when I was regularly turning cars over into ditches. So I stuck to Jaguars and the occasional Ferrari."

"Of course," I agreed, "everyone deserves an occasional Ferrari. So, do you go to Tesco in this beast?"

"Sometimes," he grinned. "I can fit a lot of shopping in the boot." He patted the car again. "This was a treat to myself, for finally sorting my life out a bit. It's going to waste, though—we'll have to do more driving. If you're up for it?" I wondered again at what point I was going to wake up and discover that everything that had happened over the last ridiculous few days had been nothing more than a dream. Maybe I had a fever and was actually lying unconscious in bed, with everyone fretting over me.

"Hello?" Marc was looking at me, his eyebrows raised. "Are you still with us?"

"Just daydreaming about fast cars," I lied. "I hope you're kinder to the gears on this than you are with the Micra."

Alice insisted on walking us to the car when we left, despite it apparently being way past her bedtime. Marc had coasted the Bentley out of the garage and it sat waiting for us in front of Heather's house, a looming hulk in the dusk. Alice clung to Marc as he hugged her goodbye and then, to my surprise, flung herself at me. I knelt down and hugged her back, trying not to notice both Heather and Marc giving it the goo-goo eyes in the background. Lovely as Alice was, I could do without a small child getting attached to me when I'd known her father for less than a week. As Alice ran to give Marc a last goodbye squeeze, Heather came up beside me.

"I know he's a lot to take on," she said quietly, as we stood watching him and Alice giggling and chasing each other around the car, "but he's a good man underneath the public image. He's made it out the other side, which is more than can be said for a lot of them." She turned and grabbed my hand, looking me straight in the eye. "But you're not to get sucked in, you hear? It doesn't matter how much me and Alice and Suzie like you and how overexcited we all get at the sheer fairytale romance of it all, you need to mind yourself. Because you matter as much as he does and it's not going to be easy. Anyway," she stepped back as Marc walked over to us, her voice getting louder again, "it's been lovely and we must do it again very soon. Now, "she looked at Marc, "give your mama a hug and get Jem home safe. Okay?" A mock stern look, which made Marc laugh.

He leaned in and hugged her tight. "Of course," he said. "This is the new me, remember?"

Heather didn't look entirely convinced. "Just do your best," she said. "That's all anyone can ask."

It was dark by the time we were back inside the M25 and heading towards Uppingwood. I was just wondering where I should ask Marc to drop me off in order to reduce our chances of being spotted, when he glanced across at me with a hopeful look.

"Would you stay with me again tonight?" he asked, his eyes already back on the road. I thought about it while he negotiated one of those appalling five-way junctions that always seem to have been invented by particularly malicious road goblins. Having safely installed the Bentley in a line of queuing traffic, he turned to look again.

I was pretty sure I was blushing. "In the hotel?"

"It's a really nice hotel," he said quickly, "don't you think? I do need to find something more permanent, though. It would be good for Alice to be able to visit and just do standard kid stuff. I'm pretty sure she thinks everyone's dad lives in a hotel suite with maids and room service ice cream on tap." He sounded sheepish. "I like being able to spoil her," another glance across at me, "but I don't want her to end up like one of those awful kids you see on reality shows, living off their parents' money and having no idea what to do with their lives."

"I think your mum would nip that in the bud pretty fast," I laughed.

"Yeah, she would," he agreed. "But still, I'd like Alice to have her own bedroom, you know? Even if it's just for holidays and the odd weekend here and there." He pulled a face. "I've got to be realistic—however much I'd like to see more of her, it's better for her to have the stability of living with her grandma and going to a village school. Hotels don't generally like their guests keeping guinea pigs in the bathrooms."

"Especially cannibal guinea pigs," I said and he laughed.

"So will you?" he asked again. "Stay with me? We could get room service and just watch movies and hang out. It would be more fun with you around."

I wondered how often Marc had been sitting alone in his room watching endless boring television when I'd been doing exactly the same in my flat. "Yes," I said. "That would be lovely." His grin in response would have been more endearing had he not taken his eyes off the road and only narrowly avoided rear-ending the car in front thanks to the Bentley's politely firm warning system. We somehow made it to the hotel without any damage to anyone else on the road—a miracle in itself, because Marc liked to talk whilst driving and kept turning to look at me when he asked questions. And he had a *lot* of questions—from my favourite subject at school (English), to my most recent book purchase (*Alice in Wonderland*, to replace the ancient battered copy that I'd had since childhood and which had finally fallen apart), via my most embarrassing moment. I told him it was when I fell over in front of a boy I liked in my second year of senior school, but it was actually a mortifying evening when I'd had one too many margaritas and passed out in a flower bed in front of a hipster pub in Shoreditch. Zoe had sweet-talked the landlord into letting me sleep it off in his flat upstairs whilst she carried on drinking.

I quizzed him in return and discovered that his favourite movie was *The Bride of Frankenstein* ('have you *seen* Elsa Lanchester? Bloody hell'), hated sprouts ('why eat tiny cabbages when you can just chop up one big one?') and liked driving big cars. Half an hour in the Bentley had me convinced that he was right on that point, at least. It cruised through the night like an elegant armoured tank, barely registering the endless potholes on the North Circular. I lay back in the passenger seat—all heated black leather and an air of luxury BDSM dungeon—and wriggled round to face him.

He glanced over again and caught me looking. "What are you staring at?" he asked with a smile.

"Just thinking about how the terrible street lighting brings out the highlights in your hair," I grinned. He shook his head and laughed as we cruised into central London.

It was dark by the time we finally pulled up in front of the hotel. A parking valet immediately appeared from around the corner and grinned as Marc handed him the car keys. I strongly suspected that they just pretended they hadn't seen him when he was driving the Micra. We headed into the small reception hall with our arms wrapped around each other and I was almost disappointed that there wasn't a paparazzi photographer lurking near the entrance to snap us for posterity. I idly wondered if it would be rude to drag Marc into bed without eating first. There was a woman standing in the expensively subdued lighting at the end of the hall, leaning back against the reception desk. Tall and angular with black hair in a sharp bob, she was dressed in skinny jeans and a leather jacket over a tight tshirt that proudly announced 'SLUT' across her chest in gold letters. Spike heels made her at least six feet tall and the general air of intimidation was increased by the fact that she was wearing huge black sunglasses indoors. Maddie was sitting at her post and pulled an apologetic expression when she saw us come in.

To my alarm, the tall woman headed straight for us. "Darling," she purred at Marc, "I was wondering when you'd get back." She leant forward to kiss him, but Marc swung his head so that she missed. She looked irritated but didn't lose her composure. "Aren't you going to introduce us?" she said, peering at me through her shades. I could see my reflection in them, which was disconcerting. Marc sighed, but didn't let go of me. I could see Maddie behind her, trying not to be too obvious about the fact that she was frantically eavesdropping.

"Hello, Rachel," he said. So this was the ex-wife. I'd been expecting a clichéd, hollow-eyed drug addict, but the woman in front of me was glossy and expensive-looking. "This is Jem,"

163

he squeezed my waist, "a very good friend of mine."

Rachel pulled off the sunglasses and narrowed her sly brown cat-eyes as she gave me the once over. "Is she now," she said slowly. "Not quite your usual type, is she Marc?" She stood with one hand on her hips. I tried not to look too fascinated with how she managed to balance on such high thin heels. Maybe she was a robot. "Something funny, dear?" she enquired archly and I realised too late that I had been grinning to myself.

"Nice to meet you" I said, and held my hand out to shake, which she completely ignored. "I've heard so much about you." Marc sniggered but managed to turn it into a cough.

"That's interesting," she replied in a tone that made it very clear that it was anything but, "I've heard absolutely nothing about you." Maddie was openly staring now—she put her head down sharply when I caught her eye, but not before she'd given me an exaggerated wink.

"What are you doing here?" asked Marc sharply. "We've said all there is to say. I need you to stay away from me now."

Rachel pouted. "Oh dear," she said, "were you hoping for some private time with your little friend?" I scowled at her. "The thing is, Marc," she stood grinning at him with her hands in her pockets, "I've been offered a *lot* of money to talk to the papers. About…things. Things that you'd perhaps rather didn't get out into the open."

"Don't do this, Rachel," Marc said quietly. "Think of Alice."

Rachel lifted her sunglasses back up and glared at him, pure hatred in her eyes. "Think of all the years that I've covered up for you, Marc Gatton," she hissed. "I bet you haven't told your little friend *everything*, have you?"

"Stop it," he said, pushing me slightly behind him as if he thought she might actually try something physical. And I wasn't entirely sure that she wouldn't—there was a faintly unhinged air about Rachel, as if she was clinging to reality by nothing more than the very tips of her glossy red, pointed fingernails. "You're going to ruin everything for all of us, not just me. Can't you put Alice first, just this once?" There was a pleading tone to his voice now, but Rachel was unmoved.

"Daughters come first, don't they, Marc?" she snarled. "At the cost of everyone else's conscience."

"That is *enough*, Rachel," Marc said, just as she moved to slap him. He grabbed her arm and held it in the air as she shrieked and started hitting him with her free hand. He pushed her sideways against the wall and leaned against her. "Maddie," he called loudly, "please can you call security?" Maddie was clearly one step ahead of him, because even before he'd finished speaking, two sharp-dressed men who looked like extras from *Reservoir Dogs* came striding out of a door to the side of the reception desk. One of them caught hold of Rachel from behind and pinned her arms to her side as she flailed angrily. She saw me standing watching the entire awful spectacle in horror and somehow found enough strength to wrench an arm free.

Grabbing my arm, she shook me hard. "He's keeping a secret from you," she hissed into my face, before the security guards managed to get hold of her again.

Marc put himself in-between us, his expression grey and broken. "We need to talk," he said to me, "but right now I'm going to have to clear this mess up."

"Don't worry," I told him. "I'm not interested in your grubby secrets, whatever they are," I turned and looked Rachel straight in the eye, "especially when they're being spilled by people who clearly left their morals in the gutter." She opened her mouth to speak, but I cut her off. "I'm not interested, Rachel. None of this is anything to do with me. I'm going to leave you to sort it out amongst yourselves." Marc tried to catch hold of my arm but I stepped out of reach. "I should go home. Give me a call when you're free." I gave him a peck on the cheek as if everything was completely normal and left them both staring after me as I walked back out onto the street. I'd have been very proud of the way I'd handled things, had I at least made it to the tube station before bursting into tears.

WHERE DO WE GO NOW, BUT NOWHERE?

Despite the late hour, when I arrived home Nancy was outside in the back garden, cutting up dead plants and pushing them into an overflowing garden rubbish bin. She looked up and waved as I unlocked the front door and I gave a half-wave back before letting myself in. I could hear noises from upstairs—Dan must be home. Shit. I'd been hoping to have some time to sort my head out before having to see him. Taking a deep breath, I headed up the stairs. The door to the flat was open and I could hear him whistling as he banged around. He was making a lot of noise, considering we had downstairs neighbours and generally tried to stay quiet. Wondering what on earth he could be up to, I walked into the living room and stopped dead. Still dressed in his work suit and standing with his back to me, Dan was pulling things off the shelves. I watched mutely as he scooped half the contents of one shelf onto the floor with a crash and then pulled the remaining half into a box on the floor. Now I was inside the room I could see other boxes, each containing books and CDs that were tumbled in on top of each other. I took another step and glanced into the bedroom. Clothes were everywhere—

some strewn across the bed and floor, others flung over the top of the bedside lamp. My clothes. Dan's were in bags near the bedroom door. Oh *fuck*. I tripped over something on the floor and the noise made him swing round to face me. He was grinning and red-faced and almost certainly drunk.

"Evening, Jemimah," he said politely, "so you finally decided to bother coming home?"

"I can explain," I began, but he put a finger to his lips and shushed me.

"No, *I* can explain," he said, stepping towards me with a precarious pile of records in his hands. The vinyl collection was his pride and joy and only usually handled with the utmost delicacy. He must be *really* angry, I thought to myself. I somehow managed to duck before the first one hit the wall behind me. Dan stood rooted to the spot, hurling albums at me as he spoke. "Had fun making a fool of me, have you?" he hissed, as another record crashed past my head. '*The Best of Jethro Tull*'—he'd obviously already packed the favourites away and had moved on to the ones he collected during his hippy student phase. "How *fucking* dare you?" *Fragile* by Yes sailed past my head. I ducked again, whilst randomly thinking that I'd quite liked that one. He was visibly shaking with anger, a limited edition Muse coloured vinyl held ready in his hand. I was pretty sure he wouldn't throw it—he wasn't quite *that* selfless. As if reading my mind, Dan glanced down at the album and put it safely on a chair, stepping towards me over the mess and tripping slightly. Recovering himself, he stood in front of me, his eyes glittering with furious tears. I put my hand out to touch him but he slapped it away. "You fucking *slut*," he hissed. I stood silently, too shocked to say anything. Dan leaned forward into my face. "Made it easy for him, did you?

Let him fuck you so you could pretend you were a teenager again whilst he tried not to notice how old and saggy you are? You filthy little bitch! He must have been desperate." Fury took over. This wasn't the Dan I'd known for years. This wasn't the Dan I'd spent so long assuming I'd eventually *marry*, for fuck's sake.

I kept my voice quiet and level. "We'll talk about it when you're sober," I said, moving to step past him into the room. Dan grabbed my arm and twisted it backwards, making me shriek with pain.

"We'll talk about it now, Jemimah," he said and leant over to grab my hair, wrenching me upright with my arm still twisted behind my back. I kicked out at him but he pulled out of the way. He pinned me up against the wall, but I managed to bring my knee up sharply into his groin and he collapsed backwards. "Fucking bitch," he howled, writhing on the floor, "you don't deserve me, you stupid cow."

"You don't deserve *her*, you mean," I spun round to see Nancy standing in the doorway, holding a pair of pruning shears in her hand. And in a distinctly threatening manner, I thought, just as Dan recovered himself enough to get up and fetch me a ringing slap across the face. "That is *enough*!" yelled Nancy and stormed past me into the room, brandishing the shears fiercely enough that he nearly fell over in his panicked attempt to back away from her. I clutched my cheek as I leaned back against the wall and watched Dan regain his balance and stand frozen to the spot, staring at Nancy with angry tears running down his cheeks. She took another warning step forward. "Get your things together and leave," she told him sharply. "You've got five minutes. Anything you can't carry, you leave in a pile and we'll have sent to the Uppy—you can collect it from there." She gave him one last shake of the shears before turning to me.

"You okay?" she asked. I nodded mutely, unable to take my eyes off Dan, who, although now openly weeping, was also already collecting his stuff together. Nancy put her arm round me, "Come on," she said kindly, "I'll put the kettle on." I let her lead me into the kitchen.

"Has he always been like this?" asked Nancy as she hunted out tea and milk in my tiny kitchen. Dan was banging around in the living room again, but at least the crashing noises had stopped.

"Never," I replied honestly. "He's always been, well…" I trailed off.

"A bit dull?" Nancy supplied helpfully. "Oh don't give me that look, you know he is." She kicked the kitchen door shut. "Not that I really care if he hears what I've got to say about him. He's *boring*, Jem." She pushed a cup of dangerously strong looking tea in front of me and sat herself down in the opposite chair, for all the world as if we did this all the time. "You're sleepwalking through life and you're the only one who doesn't see it. It doesn't matter what happens with this fancy man of yours, just use it as an opportunity to learn how to *live* again."

I sighed and stirred my tea. It was so dark that I was surprised the spoon didn't stand up on its own. "What if I'm making a huge mistake?" I looked up at her. "Marc's famous and rich and turns up in newspapers. I'm anonymous and definitely not rich and I *work* in newspapers. Not even impressive ones, either." I sighed and braved a sip of the tea. Jesus, it was strong enough to strip the enamel from my teeth. I put the mug down on the table and looked back at Nancy. "It would never work. We're just too different."

"How do you know unless you try?" Nancy looked impatient.

"Are you not even listening to what I'm saying? It doesn't matter whether it works or not. Your existence doesn't rely on a man—haven't modern magazines taught you *anything*? But you are more than equal to Marc Gatton and you need to see that." She put her mug down and glared at it. "Christ, that's disgusting. Look, it might or might not work. Who the fuck knows? Your future relationship status is irrelevant right now. But you do need to get out of *this*," a loud crashing sound from the living room proved her point, "because what *isn't* going to work is living with a Neanderthal who thinks the height of sophistication is crowing to his mates in the Uppy about how many people he's done over at work and that he's off home to knob his girlfriend." Before I could say anything—had Dan ever actually announced his knobbing intentions? I hoped not, but couldn't deny that it definitely sounded like the sort of thing he might say—the kitchen door banged open. Dan had a rucksack on his back and was struggling under the weight of two shopping bags, one toppling with clothes, the other carrying his precious vinyl. His eyes were red-rimmed with anger and tears.

"Have this," he said, throwing his door key onto the table. "Your new boyfriend might need it. I hope you come to your senses, Jem," he shifted the weight of the bags as he glared at me, "because you are going to look really fucking stupid when all this comes crashing down around you. And I'll be having a really good laugh at your expense." He kicked open the door to the landing. "We all will." We stared silently after him as he stomped heavily down the stairs, occasional sobs punctuating his footsteps.

Once we were sure Dan had left, I saw Nancy out with a promise to talk properly once I'd had some sleep and then tidied things half heartedly before giving up and going to bed. My beloved music box had fallen over and a scrap of paper caught my eye. When I picked it up for a closer look, I realised with a sigh that it was Marc's card. Or rather, what was left of it, after Dan had ripped it up and thrown the pieces everywhere. I dropped the forlorn piece of paper into the waste bin and turned off the lights, curling up under the duvet and wishing the entire world would leave me alone. Just for a little while.

I somehow got through the entire weekend without speaking to anyone. Busying myself with sorting out the last of Dan's possessions and cleaning the flat to within an inch of its life, I only switched my phone on for long enough to call Dad and confirm that yes—as always—everything was absolutely fine. Neither dad nor Jill moved in the kind of social circles that might have picked up on my extracurricular activities over the last week, so I avoided any awkward explanations. And it would be easier to tell them about the split with Dan once things had settled down a bit. I also sent Marc a brief text to say that I was taking some time out but would catch up with him soon. Hopefully the Rachel crisis would settle again, but there was nothing I could do to help and I really didn't want to get involved. I could see that I'd missed calls from both Zoe and Tris, but switched the phone back off again before I could be dragged into any further conversation. I didn't even watch television, just determinedly read books until I fell asleep each night. All those years of thinking I was addicted to the internet and it turned out that all I needed in order to go cold turkey was to have a dramatically televised affair with a rock star. Who knew?

If I'd thought that going back to work on Monday morning might bring me some much-needed normality, I was about to be disappointed. It was Tris's day off, which usually meant me working from the reception desk as cover. I looked forward to it, because the general rarity of visitors to the Mercury's office meant that I could get work done quickly before spending the rest of the day reading in peace. But to my surprise, Donna was already at the desk when I walked through the doors.

"Don't ask me," she said, before I could even open my mouth, "Arthur says he needs to have a chat with you and I'm to cover for now." Ugh. I'd already had enough of Arthur's little chats to last me a lifetime. I sulked my way through to my desk and waited for the computer to wake itself up. The Mercury didn't believe in keeping up with new technology and I was pretty sure that if Arthur had his way we'd all still be dictating to a typing pool. I was just starting on a write up of the local Women's Institute's decision to produce a nude calendar—an idea which definitely now counted as being old fashioned; plus I was desperately trying not to think about Mrs Warboys from the grocer's without her clothes on—when Arthur's door banged open. He peered around the room until his eyes settled on me.

"Can I have a word, Jem?" he jerked his head back to indicate I was being summoned. Feeling like a little kid being hauled in front of the head teacher with no idea what I might have done wrong, I got up and followed him in, ignoring curious looks from my co-workers. Arthur sat back down behind his desk with his fingers steepled and what I presumed he thought was a kindly look on his face. "Sit down, love."

I slouched into the chair opposite him and narrowed my eyes. "Am I in trouble?" I asked, "Because I'm up to date with work—I mean, I will be if I can get Mrs Warboys to look presentable before this week's edition and I know I need to file my expenses more regularly, but—"

Arthur held a hand up to stop me. "You're not in trouble, Jem." Phew. "I just wanted to have a chat about your plans." Oh.

"Well Dan leaving won't make any difference," I floundered, wondering how the hell he knew already, "and I'll actually have more time when you think about it, so maybe I should reconsider the offer of a permanent job here and—"

"I'm not talking about Daniel," Arthur said, looking thoroughly confused. "I actually thought you'd already come to your senses about him." Oh great—*now* everyone decides to tell me they'd hated Dan all along.

"I mean this Gatton chap." I looked at Arthur blankly. "You like him, yes?"

"You've lost me," I said. "What's Marc got to do with anything?"

Arthur had the look of a man who was about to have the birds and bees chat with a curious child. "I promise I'm not trying to sell stories this time," he said, actually blushing. "But, well," he stumbled, then rallied himself, "you really did look quite the couple on television last week. And I know you were out with him and his friends at that fancy place the other night." *Well thanks a fucking bunch, Tris, you terminal gossipmonger.* "Wouldn't you prefer to have some time together?"

"I'm not sure what you're saying," I said coldly.

Arthur carried on digging his hole. "Well the Mercury doesn't pay well and I thought, you know, you wouldn't need to worry about the bills if you were with him, and..." he gave up. "In all honesty, Jem," he said, "I think we're all just waiting for you to run off into the sunset with this chap of yours. And my granddaughter is looking for a start in newspapers, so…" he trailed off.

I sat up straight in the chair and forced myself to speak as politely as I could manage. "Do you want me to leave?" I asked.

Arthur shook his head vehemently. "Oh heavens no," he spluttered, "we all like having you around and you're good at the job. But," he continued, "I wanted to make sure that you knew you didn't have to feel obliged to stay."

"I like working here," I said carefully, my jaw tense, "and I'm not planning to leave any time soon. I've known Marc Gatton for a *week*, Arthur! One bloody week. Dan and I only split up at the weekend," I continued, "and the reasons behind it are no one else's business. But now I need to be able pay the bills on my own. So no, I'm not planning to leave my job, or my flat, or Uppingwood itself. Unless everyone around me continues to make my life really fucking difficult, in which case I might reconsider my decision." Arthur looked sheepish. "Now, unless there's anything else you want to discuss," he shook his head, "I have work to finish."

I seethed my way through the rest of the day, cursing Tris for not having the decency to be at work the one time I really needed a good bitching session. Arthur barely came out of his office and everyone else ignored me, presumably for fear of having their heads bitten off. When I headed out onto the street at the end of the day it was grey and raining. At least it matched my mood. I didn't have an umbrella, so just pulled my collar up and tried to ignore the damp seeping through my clothes. Hiding from a particularly vicious squall in the doorway of a closed pharmacy, I checked my phone.

No new messages. I couldn't decide whether that was a good or bad thing. Against my better judgment I finally gave in to doing an online search for Marc and felt sick as pictures began to pop up. The top result was from Twitter, which confused me for a second—I knew that Marc didn't use social media and Mike hadn't got any further than a fairly lacklustre Instagram account for Black Swans. Then I realised that it was a blurred photo of Mark and I, walking hand in hand across the woodland behind the Cheshire Cat. Those bloody women from the restaurant. Well that explained how Dan had found out—he was an avid Twitter user. I gulped a panicked breath and forced myself to keep looking.

LOVE TRIANGLE DILEMMA FOR COMEBACK ROCKER, screeched the Metro headline. I peered closely at the photo alongside the article. Marc was stalking out of his hotel with a face like thunder, followed by Rachel looking every inch the rock star wife, hair flowing and sunglasses perched on top of her head in order to better show off her glowing smile. She even had a wink for the camera. A second photo showed them getting into a black cab, although Marc clearly hadn't waited for her and was already sitting in it. The picture showing Rachel leaning in towards him whilst he stared the other way out of a window. And—oh god—there were more photos at the bottom of the article. Captioned *'What now for new love left in the dark?'* was a blurry snap of the three of us glaring at each other just inside the hotel doorway, followed by another of me stalking down the street alone, looking tired and grumpy and not at all as though I'd just had a really lovely day out. Someone must have taken it from across the street as I'd walked off. I closed my phone before I could see any more and started walking again, the rain on my face masking my tears.

I snuck in quietly when I got home, so that I wouldn't have to talk to Nancy. Lovely as she'd been, I couldn't face going over it again. I was also suspicious that she'd try to talk me into learning to meditate, or becoming one with my female energy, or—even worse—yoga classes. The one and only time I tried yoga, someone else had farted during a quiet bit of the session and I'd spent the rest of the lesson with every muscle clenched in fear of being the next culprit. I could do without that kind of relaxation. When I peered tentatively into the bathroom mirror, I found myself looking distinctly tired and drawn. No surprise there—I'd had more drama in a fortnight than I'd managed in the past thirty years. It was one thing wanting more excitement from life, but this was ridiculous. I cleaned my teeth and scrubbed my face with a flannel as if attempting to remove a layer of my skin. I made another cup of tea, pulled on my oldest, most comforting pyjamas—the ones with unicorns on them, that made me look like an overgrown child—and got into bed. Just as I was settling down under the covers, my phone pinged. To my surprise, it was Suzie. I didn't have the time or energy to get back into the drama tonight; it would just have to wait. Muting the phone, I shoved it viciously under the bedside table before pulling the duvet over my head and blocking out the world.

The alarm woke me with a jolt the next morning and I sat up suddenly, my heart thudding in my chest. After making a coffee and bringing it back to bed, I decided I'd better find out what Suzie had wanted the night before. Hopefully something minor and undramatic. That hope was short lived—rescuing my phone from the dust bunnies, I saw the screen lighting up in a firework display of notifications. I'd definitely missed something overnight. With a sinking feeling of doom I opened the phone up and started to read through. Three missed calls from Marc—flattering, but I wasn't going to think about it right now. Endless texts from Tris, which I just ignored completely because that wasn't anything new. A message from Paul, asking me to ring him back—in the middle of the night? Now I was starting to get worried. And the earliest one was a message from Suzie, which I opened warily. *What the fuck? I thought better of you, Jem. Please tell me it's nothing to do with you? S x* What was nothing to do with me? Panic growing, I opened a notification from Tris and a tsunami of messages flooded the screen.

What happened with Arthur? Donna said you had a face on all day! Cheers for that, Donna. I made a mental note to spit in her mug next time I was on coffee making duty.

Whoah. I thought you weren't going to talk to anyone about Marc Gatton? Who had I been talking to? No one who could have said anything incriminating, at least not that I was aware of. My stomach started churning nervously as I opened the next message.

Well I suppose it's up to you—I hope they paid you good money tho? Girl gotta eat, I guess. I can't believe you hadn't told me any of it tho! Catch up soon, bitch xx

I was deciding between hunting online for what Tris was talking about or just cutting out the middleman and heading to the bathroom to throw up, when the phone rang. 'MG' flashed up on the screen and I nearly dropped the phone on the floor in fright. I had no idea what it was I was supposed to have done but I was pretty sure I hadn't actually done it, so I wasn't going to give Marc the satisfaction of being ahead of me on knowledge. He could wait until I knew what was going on. I held the phone gingerly at arm's length until it stopped ringing, as if it was going to burn me.

Almost immediately it flashed with a text. *I thought we had something good going on, but clearly I was wrong. I won't bother you again. M.* Fuck, fuck, fuck. I broke the number one rule of all my friendships—never call when you can text—and rang Tris.

"Hello? Is that you, Jem? What the fuck, girl?"

I sat on the bed and nursed my coffee with the phone pressed to my ear. "I've done nothing but sleep, Tris—I haven't done anything. But everyone seems to want to get hold of me all of a sudden and that's never a good thing."

"Have you seen the Gossip today?" *Shit.*

"No." I got up and grabbed my laptop, then sat back down to open it up on the bed. "What's Kate written? I barely spoke to her, she can't have much to go on."

"You didn't give an interview then?"

Oh god, it was getting worse. I clicked through to the Gossip's website with my eyes half closed in fear. "No I bloody well—oh *fuck.*' The first item on their 'Daily Gossip' column was titled '*Marc Gatton—Our Inside Scoop On The Unknown Girl Who Rocks His World*' and was headed by a blurry photograph of the two of us standing outside the Cheshire Cat with our arms around each other. From the angle, it had been taken from inside the restaurant itself. Those bloody women. Taking a deep breath, I clicked on the link just as Tris spoke.

"Jem, look at who wrote it." I already knew the answer to that—I'd fucking throttle Kate if I ever got hold of her—but I looked anyway. I was up and out of the door before Tris could utter another word.

"What the fuck do you think you're playing at?" I screeched at Zoe across her office, my 'quietly polite fury under stress' habit clearly having hit its limits. The Gossip's teenage receptionist was flapping nervously behind me, twisting her braids with worry that she was going to be in trouble for letting me through. She hadn't had any choice in the matter. Sheer fury had propelled me out of the flat and into town, anger radiating off me so forcibly that I'd had empty seats either side of me all the way in on the tube, despite it being early rush hour. I'd made it to Zoe's office in record time and was now bearing down on her across the glossy white room as other members of staff eagerly popped their heads up above their partitions in the hope of a free show. Cynthia stood in the corner with a coffee in her hand, not even pretending to be discreet. Zoe stood up to face me, her eyes hard but pricking with tears.

"I haven't written anything that isn't true," she said defiantly.

"How do you know? Apparently Marc is enjoying a sexy fling with a blonde writer? For fuck's sake Zoe, that's *me* you're talking about, not some C-list reality show celeb! I'm supposed to be your *friend!*"

"Some friend," snickered a familiar voice behind me.

I rounded on Kate, who had appeared in the doorway behind me, a sly smirk on her face. "And you can shut it, you spiteful cow," I spat at her. "You're so far up yourself it's a wonder you can see straight. You do nothing but spend your time hanging around people who don't know who you are and wouldn't want you there if they did." She shut up. I turned back to Zoe, who at least had the decency to look embarrassed.

"It's a bloody good job we don't see each other much, isn't it?" I said. "Because you clearly can't be trusted with personal information." I was deflating now, my righteous fury sinking into hurt confusion.

Zoe rallied. "It's all right for you," she said, pulling herself up to her full height—still a good bit shorter than me, but balanced by the sheer force of her anger— "you sit around being all suburban and boring and *normal*," she said it as if it was an accusation, "only to land the man of your *literal* dreams without even trying. How have you ended up with all the excitement? This stuff's supposed to happen to *me*, not you!" I stared at her, horrified. She fought on. "I've tried to get you to come out and I've offered to take you places, but you weren't interested. And now you go and do this. I told you we could write it together, but no—you're too special for that, aren't you? Well good luck with it, is all I can say." She sat back down in her chair. "They're playboys and sharks and so far out of your league that you're going to hit the ground with a crash when he comes to his senses. Now if you'll excuse me," she swiveled back to face her screen, "some of us have proper jobs to get on with. Have fun with your new friends, Jem." There was nothing I could say to that. I stalked out of the office and rang the only person who could help me right now.

"Suzie?" I said over what sounded like war breaking out behind her, "No, don't start—I haven't done anything at all and I'll explain when I get there. We are going to need to get very, *very* drunk."

181

SINCE WHEN DID MY FRIENDS
GET SO WISE?

J ust over an hour later, Suzie was peering at me across a small table that held a pair of espressos, both of us having decided that, regardless of the emergency, ten-thirty in the morning was actually a little bit early for the pub.

"Well at least it's out in the open," she soothed. "And I've primed Paul to sort things with Marc. He can't get hold of him at the moment but I'm sure it'll be fine." She frowned slightly. "He'll get over himself."

"He rang me earlier," I said. "I didn't pick up."

"Probably for the best," said Suzie. "He's got enough on his plate just now, with Rachel threatening to tell all to the papers. He's paid her off and sent her packing back home to Paris yesterday, but we all know it's just going to keep happening. He told Paul he was going to head back over to yours to sort things out, but then he saw the headlines and it was the final straw. Apparently he went absolutely off the deep end—shouting about how he knew he shouldn't have trusted anyone, you were supposed to be different, he was going to make it work this time. Etcetera etcetera. Paul says he kept telling him you really are different, but of course Marc wasn't in the mood to listen." She patted my hand reassuringly. "He'll calm down."

I wasn't convinced. "Rachel seems to have her claws in him pretty deep."

Suzie sighed. "I guess she knows which buttons to press," she said. "And there's Alice, of course. But Marc hasn't loved Rachel for a very long time. Actually I'm not sure he's ever really cared for anyone very deeply. Until now." She raised a hopeful eyebrow.

I refused to bite. "Do you have any idea what Rachel was talking about?" I asked. "She seemed to think there was a big secret that Marc had been hiding from me."

Suzie shrugged. "His drug habit was pretty horrendous," she said, "along with his behaviour. Whatever he's told you about it and whatever you might have read in the past, it will only be the tip of what was an impressively huge iceberg. So I'd guess she's after dishing the ancient dirt out of pure spite. He's done an amazing thing in coming back from that and he wouldn't want you knowing all the gory details. None of it matters these days, anyway."

I stared glumly at my coffee. "Where do you think he might be, if Paul can't get hold of him?"

"I honestly have no idea," she confessed. "We've let Mike know what's going on," well that was just bloody marvellous, as if Wendy didn't already have enough to bitch about, "but we haven't told anyone else. There's enough in the papers already." That was the understatement of the week.

"I'm horrified that Zoe would do that to me," I said. "After all the years that we've been friends."

"People are weird," said Captain Obvious on the other side of the table. "They chase popularity to boost their own self esteem, mostly. And then when someone else does better than them, they can't handle it. You've led your life on your own terms and still ended up where Zoe would like to be—it's a hard lesson to learn."

"You think she really is just jealous?"

Suzie laughed. "Of course she is. How can she not be?" She drained her coffee. "Did I tell you I've met Zoe before?"

I looked up. Suzie was watching me with her head tilted. "No," I said, "but she did say that you two had run into each other in the past." I tipped a sachet of sugar out onto the table and drew fidgety circles in it with my fingertip. "I take it you didn't hit it off?"

Suzie laughed. "I don't generally like people who make a pass at my husband then call me a 'has-been old scrubber' when he says he's with me. She's got a sharp side to her, has your Zoe. And our marriage may have its oddities but it isn't about to be threatened by the likes of her. For all she has a glamorous life, I bet it's pretty boring most of the time. She clearly hates most of the people around her. And there's you, quietly getting on with things with your nice flat and nice job and always staying safely in her shadow. But then you turn up on television looking ridiculously hot with the man of your teenage dreams draped over you in quite an obscene manner." A snicker. "Yeah, you've pushed her nose out of joint, I'd say."

"But she's my *friend*," I wailed, close to tears.

Suzie put her hand on top of mine and gave it a gentle squeeze. "I know, pet," she said, quietly. "I know."

"You do believe that all the media crap was nothing to do with me?"

She patted my arm kindly. "Of course I do," she said. "I'm a pretty decent judge of people, Jem. I like you. And I like Marc, too. He might be behaving like a brat just now, but he really does care about you. I've never seen him act like this before now. It's interesting." She must have noticed the unconvinced expression on my face. "Honestly," she reassured me, "he'll sort himself out. He's had decades of this stupid lifestyle now and it's taking some adjusting for him to be around someone who's actually good for him." I was flattered, but shook my head all the same.

"I might be good for Marc," I said, "but I'm beginning to think Marc isn't very good for me."

"Will you come back to our house for the day?" Suzie asked hopefully. "Let me and Paul look after you?"

I shook my head. "No," I sighed, "I need to head into work. I really do need the money and I don't want to give Arthur any more ideas about replacing me. And then I'm going to go home and have a proper think about my future. It's as good a time as any to change things up a bit—I'm just not sure how."

"Something marvellous will come up," said Suzie with happy conviction. "I just know it."

Tristan caught me before I'd even made it through the office doors. As I neared the Mercury building, he was getting out of Simon's Mercedes, which was parked in one of the three spaces we were allocated down the side of the building. Simon raised a hand in greeting as Tris ran across to me.

"See you later, darling," Tris called over his shoulder, "don't do anything I wouldn't!" Simon shook his head in amusement and walked ahead of us into the office.

"Well that leaves him plenty of options," I said drily.

Tris slapped my arm. "You're such a bitch," he snarked, good-naturedly. "We both booked the morning off and had a lovely lazy morning watching old Hammer movies and having *terribly* filthy sex. Not at the same time, of course." He linked arms with me—clearly we were walking into the office together whether I liked it or not. I stayed silent until he couldn't hold out any longer. "So tell me *all* about it!" he burst out finally, "what's it really like in the Super Secret Sparkly Back Room Of Glamour?" I could actually *hear* the capital letters.

"Seriously, Tris," I looked at him, "you are so fucking predictable." He pulled a face and I relented a tiny bit. "It's nice," I said. He didn't look remotely satisfied. "It's just a bar, for fuck's sake! Even less lighting than usual and more faces you might recognise off the television," his eyes widened, "but just a bar. Full of annoying people drinking too much."

He looked disappointed. "Did you at least see any soap stars?" He looked like an eager puppy and I couldn't help but laugh.

"Not many soap stars," he looked crestfallen as we reached the door, "but quite a few from the movies." I pulled my arm from his and pushed through into the reception. Tris only just remembered to put his hand out to stop the door slamming back onto his open-mouthed face. "And if you leave me alone just for today," I called, as I backed off towards the office, "I might tell you about it. Maybe." And with that, I turned and walked into the newsroom. Arthur's office door was closed, but a faint whiff of cigar smoke said he was in and waiting for the racing to start. Steph waved a silent hello from the corner desk, headset already clamped to her ears as she tried to persuade the good business folk of Uppingwood to take enough advertising to keep us running a little while longer.

"Morning, trouble!" Neil was back from his holidays, his receding hairline nicely outlining the pink glow from his forehead. At least having had two weeks out of the country meant that he wouldn't be full of questions. He spun his swivel

186

chair around to look at me. "Bagged yourself a pop star, then?" Bollocks. Clearly my optimism had been misplaced. "Saw you in the paper, didn't I? Said to the missus, 'Bloody hell, that's our Jem' and she wouldn't believe me. Said she couldn't see you getting up to that sort of thing, but I told her we knew you better. 'Dark horse, is our Jem', I said." He swung around on the chair, grinning at me like an overgrown, fidgety child.

I sat down at my desk with a sigh. "Storm in a tea cup, Neil," I said, picking up a pile of notifications about local events from my in-tray and wondering just how many cake competitions one WI group could have. Tris had helpfully printed off an email from the local veterinary surgery, inviting me to judge 'Dog with the Waggiest Tail' at their upcoming spring show. Well, wasn't my life just a rollercoaster of excitement? I wondered what Suzie would be getting up to for the rest of the day. Probably yelling at the kids and rearranging flower displays in her amazing house. Her amazing, huge, expensive house that was way out of my league. I just hoped she could cope with having a friend who lived in the suburbs and spent their weekends looking at dogs' arses, because that was about the sum of my life right now.

I was listing the prizes for best fruitcake when Arthur came out of the office. He saw me and blushed, but to his credit he didn't take the easy option of skulking straight back into his office. Taking a visibly deep breath, he headed over and actually sat on the edge of my desk. I tried not to look too surprised at this sudden effort to be friendly and casual.

"Erm, Jem," he began, clearing his throat as I eyed him beadily, "I think I owe you an apology. Erm."

I relented. "You mean your wife has told you to apologise?" I asked.

Arthur grinned. "You know me too well," he said, relaxing. "It's never personal, you do know that?" I raised an eyebrow but said nothing. "It's just, you know…well, old habits die hard and a story is a story. You know?"

"I do know," I reassured him. "But you don't get to sell your staff's morals, Arthur." He screwed up his mouth, but I ignored him. "I've had a rough couple of weeks and I am *tired*. I want to get back to writing about flower shows and dogs' bums and how well the local Brownie group acted in their play."

"You sure about that, Jem?" Arthur didn't look convinced. "Because you seem to fit that lifestyle quite well, even if it doesn't feel that way to you. And that Gatton chap certainly looked keen enough when I saw him all over you on television." I tried not to cringe at the memory of an audience of millions bearing witness to my confusing love life. Arthur ploughed on. "Or will you get it sorted out with Daniel, do you think?"

"I absolutely will not get anything sorted out with Dan," I replied firmly. "Dan is out of my life forever and if I see him in twenty years time it will be too soon."

Arthur looked concerned. "What happened there, then?" he asked

"Absolutely nothing for anyone else to worry about," I replied. "Things weren't working out between us and he's gone. I'm fine. The last week or so has been an adventure, but it's over now and I want to get back to work. Maybe do some gardening."

Arthur looked unconvinced, but clearly wanted to be let off the hook. "Okay then," he said, standing up and brushing down his corduroy trousers, "I'll leave you to it. Make sure you check those tails out good and proper!" With a chuckle, he wandered off towards the reception, no doubt with the intention of poking Tristan for more information.

I spent the rest of the afternoon with headphones firmly plugged into my ears in the hope of giving the rest of the office the impression that I was interested in nothing other than waggy dogs and fruitcakes. Steph brought me a cup of tea at one point, which was a sign in itself that she was desperate to chat. Steph never made the tea. She'd make her own—in the chipped mug with her name on that had been a birthday present from her kids, with the milk from the fridge that had her name sharpie'd onto it—but never anyone else's. I smiled and nodded my thanks, but made it clear with hand gestures that dogs were more important than idle chat. Which, just for today, they were. Tristan plonked himself down on the desk just as I was finishing up for the day and made it clear that he wasn't going to move until I communicated with him. I reluctantly pulled out my earbuds and narrowed my eyes.

"This had better be important," I muttered.

"Nothing is more important than cake and dogs," he deadpanned. "Except, of course, the fact that you have not filled me in on anything that's been going on and I demand gossip in payment for leaving me out of your secret fun the other night." He put a hand up to silence my protests. "No, you owe me. You *owe* me, Jemimah Holliday."

I sighed. "Okay," I relented. "Buy me coffee and I'll explain all." Tristan jumped up, actually clapping his hands with glee. "You are so easily pleased," I said, rolling my eyes at him.

"Makes life easier for Simon, doesn't it?" he smirked, and sashayed out of the office ahead of me. I grabbed my jacket and followed him before Steph decided to join us.

"So?" Tris stirred the entire contents of a sugar sachet into his hot chocolate, ignoring the disgusted expression on my face.

"I don't even know where to start, other than with the fact that you'll get diabetes one of these days."

"Never mind the diversionary tactics, Jemimah," Tris sucked thick chocolate foam from his spoon with unashamed relish, "what gives with you and the ancient hottie?"

"Marc is not ancient!" Tris just grinned. "Anyway, you turn thirty next year, don't forget."

He scowled. "All right, let's drop the snark." Match point to me. "I just want to know if you're okay, Jem," he said. "Cos it's fine if it really was just a bit of public banter, but not if it's fucking up the rest of your life as well."

I sighed. "I was having fun. *We* were having fun. I like him, Tris," I looked him in the eye. "There you have it. I really like him and I thought he liked me. And maybe he does," I stirred my coffee automatically, thinking things through as I spoke. "I think he does. But I've seen him less than half a dozen times and it's already caused more grief than all the years I managed with Dan." Tris eyed the fading bruises on my arm. "You sure about that, Jem?" He raised an eyebrow. "I'm assuming that's something to do with Mr Boring?"

"I really did bang myself on a door," Tris looked unconvinced, "getting out of the way of my neighbour threatening to kill Dan if he didn't get out of my house."

He brightened up at that. "Oh, well done that woman. I assume it was the downstairs hippy?" I nodded. "Good on her. Shame she couldn't have hit him over the head with her shovel at the same time. Would have saved everyone a lot of time and energy."

"Don't say things like that!"

"Well it's true," Tristan sat back in his chair, swirling the dregs of his chocolate around in the mug. "He really was *such* a boring old fart. I have no idea how you lasted so long with him, I really don't." He signaled the waiter over. "Another hot chocolate, please love," he said. "Jem?"

"No thanks," I replied, "I'm jittery enough as it is." Tristan leant forward onto the table, steepling his fingers and looking thoughtfully over them at me.

"I think you're scared," he announced eventually, before sitting back and looking pleased with his judgment.

"Scared of what, for heaven's sake?"

"What happens when Marc Gatton comes to his senses and realises you're the best thing that could ever happen to him? Don't look at me like that, Jemimah, it's true. You are funny, intelligent and hot. Apparently. According to the straight men I know, anyway."

"Well everything's better now that I know people discuss my physical attributes behind my back," I muttered.

"Get on with you, it's not my fault that people always ask me about you just because I'm the unthreatening gay friend, now is it? Thank you, duck," the waiter placed a new mug of chocolate in front of him, "ooh and extra sugar!" He winked at the waiter, who blushed a visible rosy red as he retreated back to the safety of the cafe counter.

"See me, adding artificial sweetness to my life," Tris remarked as he stirred. "But you're as sweet as cherry pie and men know that. Idiot men like Dan who waste your time and bring you down, but also decent blokes like Marc Gatton, who've got enough confidence to let you be yourself without feeling threatened by it. So what's it going to be, Jem?" He raised a quizzical eyebrow. "Stay where you are, all safe and bored rigid, or give Marc a chance? It wouldn't be the end of the world if it didn't work out, but at least you'd know you gave it a shot. And you'll have had some fun in the meantime." I sat silently stirring my coffee way too forcefully and managed to spill it over my hand.

"Shit!"

"No need to be aggressive, pet."

I put the spoon down before I managed to stab myself with it. Through the window of the coffee shop I could see Uppingwood in all its suburban glory—flower displays, charity collectors, prim little boutiques, the lot. "You're right, of course." Tris perked up. "If I miss out on this opportunity then I'll spend the rest of my life thinking 'what if', won't I?"

He nodded. "Don't forget, love," he said, "that there's a big difference between want and need." I looked up curiously. "Well," he continued, "you might *want* Gatton in your life—and I have to say, who bloody wouldn't, I mean I know he's old but wouldja just *look* at the man," he ignored my expression, "but you don't *need* him. You can live without him, same as you can live without Daniel, King of Boredom. Or anyone else, for that matter." He put a hand on mine and I stared at it, transfixed by hearing Tristan—immature, shallow Tristan—coming out with the sort of sensible comments that Mum would have been proud of. My eyes pricked with sudden tears. "Aah come on, Jem," Tris squeezed my hand. "I know it's scary, but you need to give it a go, right?" I nodded mutely.

"And anyway," he continued, "I've always fancied myself as a groupie. Can you get me backstage?" He squealed as a well-aimed sugar sachet caught him straight in the eye.

(I DON'T NEED YOU TO) SET ME FREE

I thought about my conversation with Tris all that evening, as I tidied my already unusually neat flat. The remainder of Dan's belongings were in a couple of bin bags behind the door, ready to be dropped over at the Uppy when I could face it. Picking out dust bunnies from under the bed, I found another tiny ripped fragment of Marc's card. Perhaps I should get in touch with him and at least attempt to explain. I got as far as typing, *'Hi it's me'* into a text message, before nerves got the better of me and I deleted it. Hopefully he'd have been in touch with Paul by now, even if it was just to shout about what an awful person I was. I wondered idly what Suzie and Paul were doing whilst I kicked my heels in suburbia. Whatever they normally did, I supposed—laughing, arguing with the kids, having fun together. I used to have fun with Dan, I mused. I did occasionally wonder if I was missing out on life by staying in a safe, dull job in a safe, dull town. But life had plodded on and so had time, and eventually I'd simply got used to the routine of life in Uppingwood. But now there was nothing stopping me except myself. Before I had time to think too much about what I was doing, I picked up the phone again and called Jonty. He answered it himself, but I could barely hear him over the noise in the background.

"Who's that? Gemma? Who's Gemma? Hang on," the banging at the other end and the noise suddenly calmed down. Presumably he'd shut himself in a cupboard.

"Jem," I said loudly, "it's Jem. Jemimah Holliday. *Jonty! It's Jemimah, for fuck's sake!*"

"*Ohhh! Hello love! Hang on,*" Jonty had clearly forgotten that I could hear just fine at my end and he nearly deafened me. Holding the phone away from my head, I listened to him having a brief fight with inanimate objects before coming back to the phone. "What can I do you for, Jem?"

"I was wondering if that job offer was still open. Managing the bar? I'm pretty sure I can do it—I mean I know I can and I'd really like to, so—"

"Well thank god for that!" Jonty boomed. "Swear to god love, I am going to have a bloody aneurysm one of these days, even if it's just from keeping on top of the staff rota. Pubs weren't this complicated in Uppingwood, I can tell you that."

I laughed. "It's still just a pub, Jonty."

"Oh, you think that," he retorted, "but does the Uppy have seventeen different types of draught beer and thirty five gins with poncey bloody townies still moaning I don't have their favourite brand? How about a dozen different coffees? I think *not*, Jemimah," he said, with emphasis. "I bloody well think not." There was brief pause, during which I wondered what the hell I was getting myself into. But Jonty wasn't going to let the opportunity go. "I love it, but I definitely need help. Give Arthur a week's notice—his granddaughter can take over from you," I wondered just how many people had already known that Arthur was waiting to drop Lucy into my spot, "and I'll give you a twenty per cent raise on whatever he's paying you. Same amount of hours. You can do weekdays to start with, that'll at least give me a lie in. It'll mostly be paperwork for now, anyway. Did I tell you that I haven't done my accounts for six months?"

"No Jonty, you did not," I sighed. "And you know how crap the wages are at the Mercury. It's hardly a pay rise, considering how much travelling I'll have to do."

He snorted. "Thirty per cent then, and you can stay here whenever you like. There's a flat on the top floor that I haven't done anything with because I cannot be arsed with tenants, quite frankly. Aaah, it's all grand with the books, love—I dumped the receipts in plastic bags round to my accountant's place last week and told him to sort it out. I'll give him your number in case he needs to discuss anything. Come in next week and we'll pin down the details. Got to go!" With that he hung up, leaving me staring at the phone and wondering what the hell I'd just done. *Apparently* what I'd done was agreed to give up the only steady job I'd ever had, in favour of running a bar in the middle of one of the busiest cities on the planet. Tris would never forgive me. On the other hand, he'd now have somewhere better to hang out than the edge of my desk when he wanted gossip. It was still only ten days since my first fateful encounter with Marc, yet I'd managed to change my life completely. Not bad going, given that only a couple of weeks earlier I'd have told anyone who asked that I had everything I wanted in life. Of course, what I hadn't known back then was that what I really *needed* was for everything to change.

It wasn't that I felt guilty about leaving the Mercury, it was more that I'd made such a point of wanting to stay. And now here I was, planning to walk out on them. Not that I'd escape Tris for long—I gave it a month before he landed on my doorstep, declaring he'd always wanted to be a barman. He was on the phone when I walked into the office the next day, but everyone else turned to look at me with expectant expressions on their faces.

"Morning, love," Neil said, swivelling round on his chair. "Any more gossip for us?" Steph perked up hopefully at her desk in the corner. *If only you knew*, I thought.

I shook my head. "Sorry Neil," I lied, "all boring at this end. Maybe you should go on holiday again and give me chance to get up to something." He laughed and turned back to his work, satisfied that everything was back to normal. I spent the morning finishing up the few articles that were still left on my to-do list, whilst wondering how to approach Arthur.

He beat me to it. Just before lunch he walked in and stopped next to my desk. "You're leaving us, I hear," he said without preamble, beaming as he patted his pockets. Neil immediately swung around on his chair and gaped at us. "Can't say I'm surprised," Arthur continued, "it's about time you moved on. I spoke to Jonty," he said, in response to my confused look, finally pulling a cigar out of the depths of his corduroys with a satisfied grunt. "He says you're going to take over his place and sort him out." Bloody hell, was nothing sacred?

"I was planning to give you formal notice," I said, "unless your Lucy's happy to start straight away. I can spend a day or so showing her the ropes. And Jonty needs to keep his beak out! It's not his business to tell you even before I'd properly decided."

Arthur smiled benevolently over his glasses. "It'll do you good to spread your wings a bit, Jem," he said. "You're wasted

196

round here and you know it. A change is as good as a rest, as they say. I'll get Lucy to come in tomorrow, just see out the rest of the week." And with that, he turned and headed into his office, whistling quietly under his breath. I felt as though an unseen force had taken over and was making my decisions for me. Perhaps it really was time to let go of the reins a bit and see where the Fates took me. Life, as someone much wiser than me once said, is clearly what happens to you whilst you're busy making other plans.

TOTO, I DON'T THINK WE'RE IN
CAMDEN ANYMORE

The rest of the week flew by, not least because Lucy was not only a quick learner, she also had a million questions about everything I showed her. A small, meek-looking girl in her early twenties, she made up for her quiet appearance with a ferocious intellect and an air of determination.

"I'm not planning to stay at the Mercury very long," she confided in me, within an hour of her arrival. "It's just for my CV, so that I can apply for a internship in town." As I watched her deftly churn out three pieces on local events before I'd even finished my second coffee, I thought that Arthur might have bitten off a bit more than he could chew. Tris had immediately taken to her, because she was happy to do the coffee runs and had even offered to nip out to Greggs to fetch him a doughnut when he complained of being hungry. I suspected that the rest of the Mercury's small team would find it harder to adapt, but was pretty sure that Lucy would knock them into shape soon enough. I'd called Jonty and—after half-heartedly telling him off for dropping me in it with Arthur—agreed to start at the Old Tavern the next Monday morning. I rang Suzie as I was getting my things together at the end of the day and she picked up on the second ring.

"Hello? Jem, is that you?"

"Well I'm assuming my name came up on the caller ID, so unless I've been abducted by aliens without noticing, yes it's me." Suzie chortled. I mean, *literally* chortled.

"No need to be sarcastic, you little witch," she retorted. "What are you up to?"

"Currently I'm mostly noticing that it's quiet at your end," I said. "No kids?"

"Would you believe that they're playing outside? And they have yet to attempt to kill each other. It's a goddamn miracle," she said. "Scratch that, I've just looked out and they're dumping clean clothes into a puddle and are apparently pretending to wash them. Oh well," she said brightly, "dry cleaning bills are cheaper than nannies. Anyway, what are you up to?"

"Well I've somehow landed myself with a new job," I confessed. After waiting for Suzie's excited squealing to die down, I explained Jonty's offer.

"I love that place!" The woman was a never-ending surprise. "Honestly, I've always thought it could be a great little bar. You could work wonders there, Jem."

"I think I'm mostly expected to just herd staff and pay the bills," I said.

"Yes, yes, whatever," I could practically hear cogs whirring in her head as she spoke. "That landlord friend of yours has improved it no end, but it could definitely do with a touch of the Jem sparkle, ahaha. I shall help you, of course." Of course.

"Erm…" I began to speak, but then realised I didn't know what to say.

"Have we heard from Marc, you were about to ask?" Suzie

said and I blushed to my roots, thankful that she couldn't actually see me. "No, we haven't. And neither has Heather, which is unusual." Her voice trailed off, then brightened up determinedly. "But he wouldn't go far without seeing Alice first, so he's around somewhere. He's a grown adult, we have to trust him." She didn't sound convinced enough for my liking. "Why don't you come over?" she asked. "Have supper with us? I sent Paul out to buy meat for the barbecue as the weather's nice, but he came back with a leg of lamb that looks like it's been genetically mutated with an elephant, so he's currently attempting to fit it into the oven." Having seen Suzie and Paul's massive range cooker with my own eyes, I thought that Paul must have accidentally bought an entire sheep. "We'd appreciate the help eating it, in all honestly. I'm currently trying to bribe my vile mother to stay, as well." I heard Mo shriek with laughter in the background.

"Are you sure?" I asked. "Don't you want to make the most of having some family time?"

Suzie laughed. "With this family, the more diluted it is, the better. Anyway we can eat and drink and plan your lovely bar. And then we'll have a think about where Marc bloody Gatton might have got to."

The late afternoon sun was warm on my face as I walked up Archway Road and crossed over onto Wood Lane. As I got to the Fisher's house, Suzie's voice blared out of the tinny speaker on the entrance gate.

"I seeeeee you, Jemimah!" There was a buzz and a click as the little gate opened. I walked through and carefully latched it behind me. There was something very reassuring about shutting yourself away from the world, I decided. The side door was open, so I headed through the kitchen in the direction of both the noise and the smell of roasting lamb wafting deliciously from the oven. I found Paul flat on his back on the carpet in the family room, both kids joyously bouncing on top of him.

He waved weakly. "As you can see," he spluttered, "I am somewhat indisposed at the moment. Mo decided to go home for some peace and quiet, I can't imagine why. Get off me, you vile creatures!" The kids laughed and continued bouncing, Maude waving one arm in the air like a tiny cowboy. "Suzie's hiding upstairs, love—probably the wisest move." I stopped at the bottom of the wide staircase to check my shoes, wary of treading dirt into the pale carpet.

"Don't even bother," Suzie's voice came from above my head and I looked up to see her hanging over the bannister. "Cream was a fucking stupid idea. I'm seriously considering replacing it all with shit brown—it'd certainly cover up accidents better. Come help me?" What Suzie wanted help with was sorting out the contents of one of her three enormous wardrobes. "It's ridiculous," she said. "And more than a little bit sickening." We were surveying what looked like a high fashion jumble sale in her bedroom. "I'll give them to charity to make myself feel better. They'd make good school run outfits for the more interesting mums out there." I wasn't sure how many ordinary people were in the market for a glittery purple Versace maxi dress, but decided against bursting her philanthropic bubble. "We haven't heard from him, in case you were wondering." Suzie's voice was muffled as she struggled her way into a beaded evening gown, which, despite being full length, was a lot more restrained than a lot of the other items currently strewn across the bed. "Jesus Christ, look at the state of this!"

she stood at a side angle to the mirror and poked at her stomach in an aggrieved manner. "Too many good dinners and not enough exercise. Maybe I'll join the gym again." She flopped onto the bed. "I probably won't join the gym, let's face it," she sighed. "Perhaps I can just buy some bigger clothes. Vivienne Westwood's more flattering for curves, isn't she?"

"I have no idea," I replied drily. "You're talking to someone who feels fancy buying underwear from Next, instead of Primark."

"She is," Suzie decided, bouncing happily on the bed. "I'll go into the shop next week. I deserve new things, putting up with that rabble." She nodded in the direction of the happy screeching coming from downstairs. "It's nice to have Paul home for a bit, though. The kids only play me up because they miss him. And actually they're great a lot of the time, I just seem to always be screeching at them when other people are around. Gold parenting star to me, hey?" She looked a bit forlorn.

"For what it's worth, I think you seem like a brilliant mum," I said supportively. "It can't be easy doing most of it on your own."

"It really isn't." Suzie looked serious for once. "It's a fucking weird life, Jem. And it gets weirder once you have kids, because you can't keep up. Don't get me wrong," she said, seeing the look on my face, "I'm not worried about him leaving me. I'm the best he's going to get and he knows it." A cackle. "But I miss him. There you go—I miss Paul when he's not here."

"I miss you too, babe," Paul appeared in the doorway. "And you know damn well that I do fuck all except chaperone Mister Gatton when we're away, in the hope of keeping him on the straight and narrow. We haven't heard from him, by the way."

He looked at me.

"I think I make him cross," I sighed. Suzie threw something heavy at my head, which turned out to be a leather maxi skirt.

"You can have that," she said, "it'll suit you better than me. And you don't make Marc cross, you idiot—you confuse him. That's my theory, anyway. Isn't it, Paul?" She looked to her husband for confirmation.

He nodded. "It's taken Marc a long time to get back into straight living," he said, "and he's still not properly housetrained. Honestly, it's like being around a dog who's been mistreated—we spend an awful lot of time trying to persuade him that not everyone's out to get him."

"Except for Mike and Wendy," Suzie butted in.

"To be fair to them," Paul said reasonably, "they've stuck by us throughout all the problems. So I don't begrudge Mike his cut now that things are picking up again. Anyway me and Marc were chatting before all...this..." he waved his hands around vaguely, "kicked off, and I think we're going to go it alone as soon as we can cut the contract. We'll hire a tour manager before we do the UK next year and sort the rest of it ourselves. Yes, yes," this to Suzie, who was scrunching her face up, "we'll replace the accountants as well." He looked at me. "The accounts are currently done by a friend of Mike's," he explained, "and we're pretty sure that both he and Mike make more money out of us than they really should. So it does all need sorting out." Paul looked very much as though he didn't want to sort out anything, especially if it meant thinking about paperwork and taxes.

"Mike has to put up with you in order to afford the payments on Wendy's plastic surgery," Suzie said, rolling her eyes. "It'll be good for both of them to have their life support switched off—it's about time they learned to fend for themselves." She turned to me. "But yes, you confuse our Marc, Jemimah. He isn't used to caring about people."

I narrowed my eyes. "He's not doing a very good job of showing he cares so far."

"Yes well, we didn't say he wasn't an idiot," said Paul. "Anyway, come down and tell me about your new job whilst I cook supper. Suzie can be in charge of the drinks."

She saluted and clambered off the bed. "Aye aye, Cap'n!" She stopped and cocked an ear towards the door. "What are our darling children up to? It's very quiet." They looked at each other for a second, and then both raced down the stairs.

It took all three of us to clear up the 'cooking' that Maude and Teddy had been doing in the kitchen. There was sticky flour paste everywhere. Suzie scrubbed puddles of gloop off the floor tiles, whilst I scraped the mess off the kitchen table. Paul was scowling into a sink filled with all the utensils Maude and Teddy had been using, clearly wondering where to even start.

"Look at us," said Suzie, waving a soggy dishcloth in the air, "living the glamorous rock star life." She threw the cloth into the sink. It landed hard and splashed filthy water all over Paul, who looked as though he didn't know whether to laugh or cry. "We are getting a fucking cleaner again or I will not be responsible for my actions, so help me," she hissed at him.

"I have no problem with us having a cleaner, as well you know," Paul replied in a reasonable tone. "The trick is getting them to stay when they realise that the house is a permanent state, the kids are feral and no, we don't have Elton John and Harry Styles round for dinner on a regular basis."

"Ha," said Suzie, "not since the incident with the colander, anyway." I was about to dig for further utensil-related gossip, but Teddy chose that moment to walk in through the French windows, dripping water and soggy greenery behind him.

"I fell in the pond. Maude's still in there. She says she's having a swim."

"Fucksake."

"Mum, you promised not to say fucksake ever again. You know it's a bad 'fluence." Teddy ducked nimbly out of the way as a sopping wet tea towel flew past his head.

"Tell your sister to get out before she pees in it and kills all the frogs. Again." Teddy sauntered out casually. I suspected that this sort of thing was a regular occurrence in the Fisher household. "Come make salad, Jem," Suzie said to me, waggling a large chef's knife in my general direction. "See how exciting your life could be, if only you joined us."

"You make it sound like a some kind of cult," I grumbled, as I fished tomatoes out of the fridge and began chopping.

"It kind of is." Paul appeared in the doorway. "Once you're in it, it's difficult to leave. And only other people in the same situation really understand what it's like."

"And most of them are dickheads," offered Suzie helpfully.

"True," said Paul. "But that's because you have to be a certain level of dickhead to stick at this stuff anyway. It's a bloody ridiculous life, whichever way you look at it. And it's hard not to get sucked into the, uhhh *recreational* side of it, simply because that's often the most fun. There are only so many hotel rooms you can trash before it gets boring."

"You've never trashed a hotel room in your life," Suzie grinned. "You are far too well behaved for that sort of thing."

Paul kissed the top of her head on his way to the cooker. "And that is because I met you, my sweet," he said, leaning into the cavernous oven and pulling out a massive leg of lamb. He poked it experimentally with a knife, before putting it back in and shutting the door with a loud bang. "Everyone thought we were both mad, do you remember? Me and my drinking and you and your collectors cards." He laughed.

I look enquiringly at Suzie. "Collector's cards?"

She sighed and rolled her eyes. "I'm a collector," she said. "Or at least, I was. I like sex and I like doing it with hot fit men. Musicians generally fit the bill," a pause, "although it's usually best to avoid the bass players."

Paul hooted at that. "The voice of experience, there," he cackled. "Obviously everyone thought she was mad," he said to me, "because Black Swans were on a one way ticket to Nowheresville, fuelled mostly by me and Marc and our drinking habits. Boy, could we drink."

"And throw up, and make questionable lifestyle decisions," added Suzie helpfully.

"Yes, yes, that's enough." Paul said, waving the knife in the air for emphasis. "My only problem was that I couldn't keep standing for long enough to drink as much as I'd have liked. Marc was different, though. He was thoroughly fucking miserable and saw drink and drugs as a way to stop himself thinking about things too much. Then he met Rachel and it was doomed from there, really."

"They had Alice, though?" I tried to sound casual, but probably failed. Paul was nice enough to pretend not to notice. "They must have got on okay at some point?"

"Alice was an accident." Suzie came back in through the kitchen door. "At least, that's what Rachel always said. I have my doubts," she waggled her perfect eyebrows dramatically, "but there you go. And the girl is an absolute darling, so it's all good. And before you ask, Marc's the old fashioned type underneath it all and thought it would be better for the baby if its parents were married, so they had a quickie wedding at the registry office with Wendy and Michael as witnesses."

"Wendy wore all black," said Paul. "I think she was in mourning for the life she could have had."

"You don't mean that Wendy had designs on Marc?" I was agog.

Paul nodded, putting a large gin and tonic on the table in front of me. "Wendy would have one hundred percent walked out on Mike had Marc shown the slightest bit of interest," he said. I sat silently staring into my drink, "but he didn't. So she installed Angie into the management side of things, presumably in the hope that Marc would take up with her instead. Keep it in the family and all that."

"Well that's all very nineteenth century," I said. "Whatever happened to bloody self respect?"

"Angie would be a nice kid if Wendy didn't use her as a pawn," said Suzie unexpectedly. She saw the expression on my face. "Seriously Jem, she just has an issue with you because you're a threat. She's protective over our Marc, which is ironic given that her own bad habits come from trying to keep up with him. She doesn't want anyone upsetting the status quo, which is a risk if Marc takes up with someone. And you are that someone," she waggled her glass in my direction, "and it isn't proving easy. However," she grabbed the wine bottle from Paul as he walked past and topped up her glass, "darling Marc is a fully grown adult. If he can't cope with the stresses and strains of real life, then that's on him, not you."

We installed Maude and Teddy in the family room with pizza and kids' television, carefully propping the door so that we could keep an eye on what they were doing. The three of us sat at the big kitchen table and Paul dished up ridiculously huge piles of meat alongside baked potatoes and salad.

"Well at least *some* of it's healthy," he said, shrugging. I stared down at my plate, wondering again at the speed at which my life had changed. Less than two weeks earlier I hadn't even met the Fishers, yet here I was sitting down for tea with them as if it was the most normal thing in the world.

"Marc really is a brat," said Suzie, interrupting my thoughts. "Don't try to defend him, Paul," Paul made a gesture that I was pretty sure translated as him not being about to defend anyone and that he would, in fact, agree with what was being said, if he wasn't too busy eating, "I know he's your friend but he needs to grow the fuck up." She waggled her fork at him for emphasis. "I love him dearly, but I see his faults. He's had years—*decades*—of people doing what he wants when he wants, and that warps a person. You're lucky you've had me to keep you on the straight and narrow."

Paul snorted. "You mean we balance each other out," he winked at her.

"That too," she agreed, "but you're committed to me and the kids and that makes a difference. Marc's never really committed to anyone except Alice. And even she isn't a day-to-day responsibility for him. What he needs is—" My phone rang loudly, making us all jump. I scrabbled in my bag for it and brought it out held at arm's length, as if it might explode at any second.

"It's Zoe," I said, still staring at it.

"Just answer it, Jem," said Paul. "Maybe she wants to apologise." He didn't look convinced. I was still staring it when Suzie helpfully leaned over and poked the answer button

208

with a well-manicured talon. Staring at her in horrified fury, I tentatively held the phone to my ear.

"It's me," said Zoe unnecessarily. I didn't reply. "Are you there, Jem? I need to speak to you."

"I'm not sure what we have to say to each other," I finally said.

I heard Zoe take a deep breath at the other end. "Look, you can hate me if you like, but I'm trying to help." I snorted. "Jem, I honestly don't blame you for hating me, but let's worry about that later. I've just seen Marc."

"Where did you see him?" Suzie and Paul both snapped to attention.

"In the World's End." Somehow I didn't think Camden was Marc's usual drinking area of choice. "He was with that Angie woman. Which is absolutely none of my business, obviously, but he didn't look well and I don't think he's making very good decisions right now. Mostly because he's very recognisable and is currently getting determinedly drunk in one of the busiest pubs in town. Anyway," she continued, "I thought I'd let you know before the paps get wind of it." And with that she rang off.

"He's still not answering," Paul looked frustrated as we headed out of Camden tube and onto Kentish Town Road. Leaving Suzie at home with the kids, we'd had no option but to take the tube. However much Zoe's call had sobered us all up, we'd still had several glasses of wine each before she rang and no one was in any fit state to drive. The World's End glittered in the early evening light, already loud and busy. "Nigel!" Paul hollered at a huge man who was supervising the pub's door. He grinned broadly and came to greet us as we crossed the road towards him.

"Hey, man," Nigel slapped Paul's arm and then hugged him in that way that involves a lot of macho back-thumping. "You looking for Marc? He's long gone, mate." He looked at me curiously but said nothing. "Headed off to the Black Heart, I think he said. I say 'headed'—he was being propped up, pretty much. Short blonde bird, looked a bit familiar."

"Bloody hell," said Paul, "what the fuck's he playing at?" Nigel shrugged. "Cheers though," Paul continued, "appreciated." They thumped each other again and Nigel gave me a friendly half-wave.

"Good luck," he said to me. And as I turned my back, "You'll need it."

We drew a blank in the Black Heart, a pretty Irish barmaid telling us brightly that she knew exactly who Marc was, of course she did, but she was used to weirdness in her bar so just served them and didn't ask questions.

"I think it was more than the drink he'd been having," she said, "if you know what I mean. And they left after the one."

"We'd better try Angie's place," said Paul when we got back out onto the street. "It's only five minutes from here, I reckon that's where they'll have gone." I walked silently beside him as he headed off determinedly down Greenland Road and onto Parkway. My assumption that Angie would live in some kind of squat above one of the shops on the High Street was proved mistaken, as we turned onto Arlington Road.

"Does Angie share with friends?" I asked. Paul snorted.

"No one would put up with her for long," he said. "Nah, mummy and daddy let her stay in their place when they're out of town. And she's away with us a lot of the time anyway. This way." He took a sharp left at the Good Mixer and onto

Inverness Street. The standard of the buildings was improving rapidly as we walked on, Camden gradually turning into Primrose Hill.

"It's a bit more upmarket than I'd expected," I muttered.

Paul laughed. "You ain't seen nothing yet," he grinned. We got to the end of the street and Paul took a sharp right, finally stopping in front of a house that had no name or number. Steps led up over the basement, to a white door with three neat bells on it. No dingy squats for Angie, then. I stood shivering on the steps as Paul rang each bell in turn. He'd just lifted his hand to hammer on the door itself when it opened from the inside and a small, frowning Chinese woman appeared.

"Can I help you?" she asked in a cut glass accent. She squinted at Paul. "Oh," she said flatly, "it's you." Paul and I looked at each other quizzically and then back at her. "You're a friend of Mr Gatton's, yes?" Paul nodded. "Then you might like to ask him and Miss Goldren to keep the noise down. *Some* of us have to work in the morning." With that, she stalked off down the hallway, leaving the door open for us to step inside.

"She's new," said Paul. "Mind you, I haven't been here for ages. Suzie doesn't like it."

"I can't imagine why," I followed him into the hallway, which was thickly carpeted with red plush. I didn't bother checking the bottom of my shoes, this time—somehow I didn't mind quite so much if my boots traipsed mud in on Angie's floors. Paul headed up the stairs, so I closed the front door and took a deep breath before setting off after him. Angie's flat was on the top landing, the front door left carelessly open onto a tiny entrance hall decorated with black damask wallpaper and matching dark gloss woodwork. The glam-goth effect was marred slightly by the empty beer cans and vodka bottles strewn across the carpet.

"Here we go again," Paul sighed, and pushed the inner door. It swung open on well-oiled hinges, revealing a scene of absolute chaos. The living room had been grand, once upon a time. Its height and ornate cornicing would have made it feel airy and open, had the curtains not been pulled tightly closed. Paul flicked a switch and a huge but very dusty chandelier in the middle of the ceiling suddenly lit the room in depressing detail. Antique furniture was covered in stains and cigarette burns. Takeout food cartons and overflowing ashtrays littered all the available surfaces and a pile of filthy clothing and blankets was strewn across the floor. Paul gave it a kick and it groaned. Leaning over, he pulled a young and scrawny white man up onto his knees. "Get the fuck out of here, you freeloading bastard," he hissed. The man scrambled upright, backing away and holding his hands out in the universal 'calm down' gesture. His hair was matted and, despite having just been woken up, he looked like he hadn't slept in days.

"Okay man, okay," he muttered, looking around him as if for his belongings. He settled for a half empty cigarette packet from the mantelpiece and a bottle of wine that he unearthed from underneath the heavy oak coffee table, before sidling past me towards the door. "Dunno what your problem is, mate," he said when he was safely past us at the top of the stairs, "you need to learn how to have fun." With that, he ran down the stairs and banged out of the front door, leaving it to slam back against the house with a thundering jolt.

"Close the front door," Paul said to me as we heard the downstairs neighbour emerge. I kicked it shut before she could decide to come up and give us a lecture. I was just about to question him about the positioning of such a shit

212

heap in an area as genteel as this—Alan Bennett lived round here, for god's sake, surely there should be some rules about standards—when a figure appeared in the dim hallway that led off the main living room.

"Ahahahahah, if it isn't the village idiot," snorted Angie through a mess of tangled hair. She had a vodka bottle in one hand and looked as though she hadn't slept for a week. "Come to rescue your Prince Charming?"

"Pack it in, Ange," said Paul sharply. "The only thing Marc needs rescuing from is himself. And possibly you," he looked her up and down. "Does your mother know you're in this state again?"

She snorted. "My parents don't give a fuck," Angie spat, "and you know it. My darling mother is just a gold digging slut who'll follow anything in a pair of designer trousers. A bit like your little friend, here." She glared defiantly at me.

"Tell me where Marc is, you sour-faced little cow," I hissed. Angie leant against the kitchen worktop, knocking a pile of unwashed crockery that fell to the floor and smashed everywhere. She ignored it and lifted the bottle to her lips, taking a deep pull of vodka before she spoke.

"He's safe enough," she slurred. "He'd gone out drinking on his own, so I went to find him. He wouldn't stop wailing about darling Jemimah here, so I gave him something to calm him down. At least he's quiet now."

"Get in the front room and bloody well stay there," Paul ordered. Angie didn't move, but she did at least shut up. "Come on," he said to me, heading to an opposing pair of doorways at the end of the hall. One was open onto a room filled with clothes rails. To my surprise, they were all filled with glittering dresses and designer outfits. Along the back wall were racks of shelving, crammed with handbags and shoes. Strewn across the floor were endless jeans and t-shirts, with stained underwear dotted around amongst the mess. It was like some kind of weird art installation. "This one, then," said Paul and pushed the opposite door with his shoulder. It opened easily and he nearly fell into the room, stumbling over more empty bottles and a discarded jacket that I recognised as Marc's. The curtains were open and we could see that there was no bed in the room, just a filthy mattress lying on the floor in the corner. A duvet was draped over something vaguely human-shaped. Paul gingerly tiptoed through the minefield of rubbish and poked at the lump on the grotty, makeshift bed. "That you, mate?" No response. "Gonna wake up and let us know you're not dead?" It should have been a joke, but it didn't sound much like one.

"I'm not trying to steal him away, you know." The voice came from the hallway behind us and I turned to find Angie leaning unsteadily against the doorframe. She'd wrapped herself in a scraggy dressing gown and was smoking a cigarette, the ash dropping onto the carpet. She looked me in the eye. "I was looking after him."

"What?" I asked. "How does this count as looking after him?" Angie sighed and tried to walk closer, but stumbled and decided to stick within the safety of the doorframe.

"You all think I'm in love with him," she said, "don't you?" She snorted. "And I have to live with that, because I'm not allowed to tell anyone the truth. Anyway," she waved her cigarette in the air, "I'm done with covering up secrets. Thing is," there was another wobble and she slid down a few more inches, "none of you know the real reason why I'm so devoted to that idiot." A loud snorting laugh that sounded as though it might turn into tears. "Well, I'll tell you. Then I'm going to stand back and watch the shit hit the fan and I am going to *enjoy* it, because I am sick of being a grubby little secret. You want to know why I hang around him so much? Like a little lost sheep? He," she pointed a wobbly finger at Marc, who was now groaning slightly in response to Paul's questions, "he is…ahahahhahahaa…"

"Fucking *hell* Angie," Paul spat, turning round to look at her, "will you just blurt your big fucking secret and be done with?" But I had a horrible feeling that I knew where this was going. Angie leaned back at the wall and gazed at me, tear-streaked eyeliner running down her cheeks. She nodded at me, seeing the realisation dawn on my face.

"Yup," she said, twisting her face up into a pained expression, "I'm his daughter."

"But you're Wendy's daughter!" Paul had stood bolt upright when Angie had dropped her bombshell and was now staring at her in horrified amazement. "Wendy and Mike's daughter. Mike was our manager before you were even born!"

"I'm Wendy and Marc's daughter," Angie said slowly, "not Mike's. Would you believe that Mike doesn't even know? I found out before he did, ahahahah." She slid jerkily down the wall and slumped in a heap, her head leant back and her eyes closed. "You thought I might have led him back down the wrong path, didn't you?" Her eyes opened just enough to squint at me angrily. "As if I'm the bad influence. A bad influence on Marc fucking Gatton, of all people. He's perfectly capable of ruining everything with no help from me. She slid another few inches down the wall and fought to get back upright, sighing heavily. "He's fine," she said. "Had too much

215

to drink and he isn't used to it, so he started getting loud and stupid about how you're too good for him and how he always fucks everything up. He wouldn't shut up, so I told him he was right on all counts, dumped a diazepam in his drink and brought him back here to have his breakdown in private." With that, Angie's eyes closed and she slid down onto the floor. I stepped across and pulled her upright, before turning to Paul.

"One thing at a time," I said. "Help me get her somewhere more comfortable." Paul headed out of the door and I heard him thumping around for a minute before he reappeared.

"I've cleared a space on the floor in the other room," he said. "Chucked a blanket on it so she's not on the disgusting carpet." He saw my confused expression. "If we put her to bed," he explained, "she might suffocate. Floor's safest. Believe me, I've done this more times than I like to remember." With that, he grabbed Angie's other arm and, between us, we dragged her into the spare room. After lying her down on the blanket in the recovery position, I grabbed a throw that was hanging over one of the clothes rails and draped it over her. She drowsily pulled it up over herself and smiled, although her eyes stayed closed.

"I think actually like you, Jem," she said. I gaped down at her, but she still didn't open her eyes. "You might be good for him. And I'm pleased it's all out in the open now." There was a sort of half snort and half choke, and then she almost immediately began snoring. Parking all the new information at the back of my mind for the simple reason that I hadn't a fucking clue what to do with any of it, I followed Paul back into the bedroom. Sitting down on the mattress, I felt something sticky under my backside and grimaced. Oh well, it would come out in the wash. Probably. I pulled the duvet back to reveal Marc's drawn face. His eyes were tightly shut against the sudden brightness and he groaned as he shifted slightly. Putting a hand on his shoulder, I gave him a gentle shake.

"It's me," I said. "Jem. Are you okay?"

A faint smile cracked the edges of his lips. "I thought you'd never arrive," he mumbled.

Paul leaned over me to inspect him. "Fucking hell, mate," he said, "what a state to get into." He lifted the duvet then immediately dropped it again. "And you don't appear to have any clothes on."

"I was sick," he mumbled. "Can't sleep in icky clothes."

Paul rolled his eyes. "You get into this kind of state and worry about what clothes you're sleeping in? You need to sort your priorities out." He turned to me. "Can you give Suze a ring and tell her what's happening? I'm going to get his royal twatness here checked out by an expert." I moved to stand up, but Marc shot out a surprisingly strong hand and grabbed my arm.

"Don't leave me, Jem," he said, before his hand dropped and he lost consciousness.

"I thought he'd given all this up?" The doctor waved a hand around to indicate the 'all this' that surrounded us.

"So did I, doc," said Paul. He'd made a call whilst I was having a whispered conversation with a relieved but furious Suzie and within minutes, a very quiet and very expensive car had pulled up outside Angie's house. Paul had gone down to open the front door, determinedly ignoring the indignant questioning of the downstairs neighbour. Briefly introducing himself to me as the rather unlikely-sounding Dr Zep, the doctor had opened up his old-fashioned leather bag and was currently kneeling over Marc, taking his blood pressure and attempting to get coherent conversation out of him.

"Everyone needs a pet physician," said Paul, when I asked him about the mysterious mobile medic, who had banished us to the kitchen in order to give him and Marc some space. Angie was still snoring on the floor, after Zep had checked her over and declared her safe to be left sleeping it off. "Well," Paul clarified, "you do when you're in our position, anyway. Can you imagine someone like Marc going to a local doctor's surgery? You'd only need one blabbermouth in the waiting room and suddenly the entire world would know all about your ingrowing toenail and that dairy gives you the shits."

"Well, when you put it like that," I said, "how could anyone resist the glamour of being a doctor to the stars?"

Paul laughed. "Even famous faces get yeast infections," he winked. "And you don't want to know how awkward it can be when a fan gives you the clap."

"You're right," I said. "I don't want to know," but Paul was undeterred. "Aah, it's a long time since his lordship in there," he nodded towards the bedroom door through which we could hear Zep murmuring firmly to Marc, "has been up to any of that kind of stuff," he said. "He just hasn't been interested since he split up with Rachel and finally got clean. Not because he was tragically upset about Rachel," he said reassuringly, "it's more that he didn't want to risk getting hurt again. And, of course, Alice took precedence and no one else was going to get a look in. Well," he gave a wry smile, "that's until you turned up, of course." I sighed and Paul tilted his head to look me straight in the eye. "That's assuming that you feel the same about him in return, of course."

"I really like him, Paul," I said, looking him straight in the eye. "I mean, I *really* like him. We're talking 'breaking up with my boyfriend and reassessing my entire life' levels of liking him. "

Paul laughed. "In that case," he said, "you are in *real* trouble."

UNEXPECTED GUEST IN THE BEDROOM AREA

"He's still asleep," I said, phone clamped awkwardly between my ear and shoulder as I attempted to do the washing up whilst talking to Suzie. "Is he really supposed to be so quiet?" Dr Zep had jabbed Marc with several unknown substances before declaring him 'overtired'—my suggestion that this was the biggest understatement I'd ever heard in my life was professionally ignored—and recommending that we take him somewhere quiet to sleep it off. As the Highgate house couldn't be described as quiet by anyone's standards, Paul had suggested driving Marc over to my place. When I resisted, he'd pointed out that my suburban flat was the last place anyone would look for a famous musician and it therefore made sense for me to put him up 'for a night or two.' By the time Marc had been dressed in an oversized pink tracksuit that Paul had found at the back of Angie's clothes rails and then manhandled into the good doctor's car in order for us to set off on the lengthy journey out to Uppingwood, he was starting to look better. This recovery had been helped in no small part by him having been violently sick on Angie's carpets just before we left.

"I'll send a cleaning team in," Paul had said. "And when he's awake, we'll have to discuss the Mike issue. But until then, it's between us and Angie." Marc had woken up for long enough to peer out of the car windows and mumble in confusion before making himself comfortable on my shoulder and going to sleep. "He'll be like that for a good few hours," said the doctor, and I wondered briefly why I didn't take a sleeping pill on the rare occasions I had a hangover. It clearly made the process more bearable. I was stroking his hair absently as Paul turned round to talk to me.

He'd grinned. "You make a nice couple," he'd said. "Seriously." I'd smiled a faint response, then gone back to staring out of the car window as the city became fractionally greener and we headed into the wilds of Uppingwood. Dr Zep and Paul had somehow managed to get Marc upstairs and into my flat without anyone seeing us, helped by the fact that it was now the middle of the night and hardly anyone was around. Nancy and Sid's place had been in darkness as we made our careful way to my front door. Marc could just about stand upright, but needed the support of both men propping him up in order to move around with any accuracy. "Where would you like your parcel delivered, Miss?" Paul had asked with a chuckle when they finally staggered in through the upstairs entrance to the flat.

"Just put him to bed," I pointed them in the right direction. "I'll sleep on the sofa tonight."

"No you bloody well will not," Marc had mumbled. "We have to talk."

"You can talk to the lady tomorrow," Dr Zep had said, lowering him onto my bed and pulling his shoes off, before swivelling him round and tucking him in. Marc looked like an oversized toddler in his pink babygro. I hoped Zep was on a decent retainer in return for having to act as on-call nursemaid to people who ought know better. Paul had gone back into the living room and was talking to Suzie on the phone.

"Yes, he'll live. I know, I know, he's his own worst enemy." A pause. "Aah, she'll be fine, she can handle him." A wink at me. "Not that he's capable of being handled much, at the minute." I heard Suzie laughing at the other end. "Yeah, I'll arrange things for Angie on the drive back into town. Zep's going to give me a lift. See you soon, babe." He'd cut off the call and turned to me. "She says she'll call you later. And that you need a bloody medal for patience." When he finally stepped forward and gave me a hug, I clung to him like a life raft. Eventually he'd given me one last squeeze and then peeled me off. "You have my permission to kick him into the middle of next week when he wakes up," Paul assured me. "He deserves it. Give him hell, girl." With that, both men had disappeared down the stairs. I heard the car roar into life and fade away, before heading into the bedroom to check on Marc. He was lying on his side in the spot where Dan used to sleep. But it didn't seem weird, just…*normal.* Just Marc lying there, as though this happened all the time. I decided to leave him alone for a bit longer whilst I found something constructive to do, which is why I was carefully washing up a single plate and mug when Suzie rang. As I picked up the phone I realised that it was gone one in the morning.

"Paul's already been giving Wendy hell," she announced, "but hasn't mentioned that we know the big secret. We need Marc to be conscious before we deal with that one. Anyway, he told her that she has a responsibility towards Angie and has been shirking it for years. I yelled that she should use her Botox money on a therapist for her bloody daughter, but I've no idea if she heard me say it." A muffled voice in the background. "Oh, apparently she definitely heard it. Ha!" a note of glee crept into her voice, "it's about time that old witch got pulled back into line. Anyway," she remembered what she'd actually called for, "how's our sleeping beauty getting on?"

"I keep going to check his breathing, like in the movies," I said. "He's so still that I keep thinking he's dead. I cannot have a dead celebrity in my bed, Suzie," she snorted, "the last couple of weeks have been stressful enough as it is."

"Calm down," she soothed. "Don't forget that the rest of us have seen this many times before. He's just a bit older now and it'll take him longer to get over it. Silly boy."

"He's in my bed," I said. "Do you think it would be unethical if I got in with him?"

"I think he'd like nothing better," she assured me. "And I'm sure it would be healthier for him to keep warm and comforted."

"Huh," I replied. "I don't know about comforted. Marc and I have done nothing except misinterpret each other since the first time we met."

"You're a pair bloody-minded idiots," Suzie said reassuringly. "Probably better to stay with each other, instead of inflicting your ridiculous selves on anyone else. Anyway," I heard Paul in the background, "apparently Teddy has got out of bed and is doing inadvisable things to Mr Bean, so I'd better go. Promise to ring me in the morning?" I promised, and then hung up. It immediately rang again. I stared at it until it went quiet, and then rang the number back before I could change my mind.

"Have you found him?" Zoe spoke quietly, but there was a note of genuine concern in her voice.

"Yes." A pause. "Thank you."

"You're welcome," she said, and then sighed. "Look Jem," she said, "for what it's worth, I'm sorry. I was an idiot. You don't do that kind of things to friends. I was—I don't know," she thought about it for a moment, "well, I guess I was jealous. It was just unexpected, you know?"

"What, that I might be capable of having an interesting social life without you organising it for me?" Silence at the other end.

"I deserved that," she finally said. "And for what it's worth, yes. I'd been the one with the interesting life for so long, you know? And I'd got used to you not wanting to be involved. So I didn't know how to handle it when you suddenly appeared on my territory—and you clearly didn't need me." A long pause. "Can we still be friends?" I thought about it for a long moment. About Zoe always trying to expand my horizons, and also about her holding my hand that day in the crematorium and knowing just how to pull me through.

"Yes," I said finally. "We're still friends. But Marc is off limits. I won't talk about him and you won't ask. Deal?" I could practically hear the cogs whirring in her head before she finally gave in.

"Deal," she said. "I slapped Kate, for what it's worth," she added, making a muffled snorting noise. "Thought I'd lose my job, but apparently they like a bit of bitch-slapping over at the Gossip. Anyway, she walked out in a fury when no one stood up for her and now there's a job vacancy." A pause. "Don't suppose you fancy working at a trashy mag? You don't have to talk about your boyfriend, ever," she said, "but I reckon you probably know your way around a celebrity bar these days." The job offers were coming thick and fast this week.

"I don't know, Zo," I said finally, "but I might be able to get you into an interesting club I know. You just have to promise to be nice to Tristan."

Dawn was threatening to break by the time I pulled a spare duvet out of the airing cupboard in order to make myself comfortable on the sofa. I padded quietly into the bedroom to find some nightclothes. Marc was still out cold and, according to Dr Zep, would stay that way until the morning, at least. I wriggled out of my jeans and slid a drawer open in the hunt for pyjamas.

"Nice view," croaked a familiar voice behind me. I spun around. Marc hadn't moved an inch, but one eye was open and squinting to focus on me. "We're still friends, then?"

"That's the second time tonight that someone's asked me that question," I said.

Marc gave me a wry smile. "I'm sorry," he said, "I haven't meant to mess you around. But it works both ways, you know? You just walked out that night when Rachel appeared and the next thing I knew, our story was appearing in the gossip columns." He rolled over onto his side, groaning. "Fucking *hell*, my head hurts. Anyway, what was I supposed to do?"

"Not assume the absolute worst of me without giving me chance to explain first?" I suggested.

He groaned again. "I know," he mumbled, "I am an appalling human being and I don't deserve you. Or Paul, or Suzie...or anyone else who's stuck by me." He scrunched his eyes up tight.

"You can stop with the hair-shirt bollocks, Marc," I said, "there's more important things to discuss right now." He didn't say anything. "We know about Angie," I continued. One eye blinked wide open at that, so I ploughed on. "She's a good kid and she shouldn't have been put in this position. What were you *thinking*, Marc?"

He groaned. "About what?" he mumbled, "hiding Angie? Or sleeping with Wendy decades ago when I was too off my head to even know what I was doing? I didn't even know I was Angie's father until a few years back—I was so shocked that I made the mistake of telling Rachel about it. I needed a bit of support and I couldn't bear to tell Paul or Suzie because I knew they'd be horrified. So now Rachel has something to hang over me whenever she's in need of rescuing."

"Well it's going to come out now," I said, "and it's about time. It's no bloody wonder Angie's such a mess, Marc!" A thought occurred to me. "How did you find out she was your daughter?"

Marc sighed. "Someone bought her one of those DNA test kits for her eighteenth birthday," he said, "and it came back without any Irish in it whatsoever. Which was a surprise, because Mike's family is almost entirely from County Wexford. Anyway it was put down to being a weird freak of genetics, but Wendy knew there was a possibility that Mike wasn't Angie's father. So she asked me to take a paternity test." He coughed and groaned. "Fucking hell," he mumbled, "my head's killing me."

"Good."

"You're a horrible woman," Marc muttered, but he was trying not to smile. "Anyway I freaked out, as you can imagine, but then I did the test. Wendy didn't used to be an awful person," he said, "not back then. We were both sad and lonely and that's when things happen, isn't it? It was a one-off and we agreed to pretend it had never happened. And that's what we did, until a stupid novelty gift blew the lid off everything."

"Does Mike have any idea at all?"

Marc grimaced. "No," he said, "he doesn't. Wendy told Angie that the second test was just more DNA stuff, I think. When the results came back I spent about a week having a fairly constant panic attack about it all, which is when I ended up telling Rachel. And then I spoke to Angie. Probably the wrong thing to do, but I felt she deserved to know. She was still just a kid really and she didn't want to risk ruining everything, so we just…carried on, as if it hadn't happened. I shouldn't have told her at all, with hindsight, because it left her with a huge mental weight to carry. But I didn't want her to suspect things and then worry that I didn't care about her, you know? As it is, I suspect that some of the crew have known for a while, because none of them have ever questioned the fact that Angie spends a lot of time with me. I guess they like her more than they like Mike." He shrugged and winced. "I'm glad it's out in the open," he said, "because I'm sick of hiding things. Really I am. I spent years hiding my drinking and then even more years hiding my drug habit. Then I did a stint of hiding just how bad my wife's drug habit was, until she decided to run off with her dealer and I had no one left to take drugs with. And, well, it got boring then, if I'm honest." One eyelid cracked open and he looked at me. "So I got clean and I got back on the road and it was still all pretty boring—until I met you."

I sighed and sat back against the pillows with my feet hanging off the edge of the bed. "Didn't you say that Angie knows more than anyone about how this business works?" I asked him. A mumbled agreement. "So make her your tour manager," I continued. "You and Paul can get new accountants and sort everything else yourselves. Take some control back. And let

Angie do the really difficult job. She'll be good at it."

Both eyes opened this time. "You're not kidding, are you?" I shook my head and Marc grinned. "Since when did you get so wise, Jemimah Holliday?" he asked. "Anyway," he patted the bed next to him, "how about getting in with me and saying hello properly?"

'Talk about in at the deep end," I sighed and sat down on the edge of the bed. Marc absent-mindedly stroked my thigh and I swear to god my entire body shivered. "Also, you stink."

"Not exactly a prize catch, am I?" he said mournfully. "But I promise faithfully that I really do think you are bloody marvellous and I plan to make all of this crap up to you. But right this minute, I need to sleep." The hand slid further up. "Come curl up with me?" I stripped down to my t-shirt and knickers, and then wriggled down into bed with my back to him. I hadn't been joking about the smell—legendary rock star or not, his breath was absolutely rancid. He automatically reached for me, pulling up tight behind me and wriggling against my back. Whatever Zep had said about him being out for the count for a while, that clearly didn't apply to certain parts of his anatomy. But I was too tired to do anything other than sleep, curled up with Marc's arms wrapped tightly around me like a prize he was never letting go.

ABSOLUTE BEGINNERS

Whyen my alarm went off the next morning, I couldn't make my hand move to hit the snooze button. Claustrophobic panic built for a second before I realised there was a heavy arm draped over me. I managed to wriggle free and switched the racket off, before lying back down and waiting for the adrenalin to settle. Marc was breathing slowly and steadily next to me, sounding far healthier and more stable than he had the night before. I didn't want to get up, but neither did I want to be some sap who gave up on everything else when a man was on the scene. He mumbled as I slid out of bed, but didn't wake up. Even running the shower and boiling my ancient and very noisy kettle didn't disturb him. I drank my coffee sitting on the sofa, positioning myself so I could watch him lying peacefully in my bed through the doorway. As I packed my bag for the walk into work, I remembered that I'd tucked Dan's door key away on the top shelf in the kitchen. After removing the plastic fob—I was pretty sure Marc could live without being known as 'Dan the Man'—I stepped quietly back into the bedroom, where he was curled up on his side and sleeping like a baby. In the morning light coming in through the thin curtains, he looked a good decade younger than he actually was. I placed the key quietly on the pillow by his head and left.

"Are you sure you're going to be okay without me? Perhaps I should work a longer notice period?" I was sitting in Arthur's office, fretting in the face of my soon-to-be-ex boss's complete lack of concern. It was the end of what was supposed to be my last day at the Mercury and I was suddenly terrified. Being press-ganged into giving only two days notice on a job you've done for years will do that to a girl. It didn't help that I was absolutely exhausted after the previous night's activities and, however much Zep and the Fishers had reassured me that he'd be fine, I couldn't relax until I'd got back home to check in on Marc. "It wouldn't hurt Jonty to wait another week or so," I went on, "he's managed this far."

Arthur smiled kindly at me. "Oh come on, Jem," he said, "you've been here too long as it is. You're thirty, not sixty! Get out in the world and explore a bit. Never mind what happens with that singer of yours, you've got time to find yourself lots of different men. Or women. Both, maybe."

"Arthur!" He'd never struck me as someone who considered anything other than a straight, monogamous relationship the way forward.

He grinned. "Oh, I read the papers," he said. "You youngsters have more freedom than we ever did and you'll regret it if you miss out. One day I'll tell you about a very lovely young chap I once met in Greece." Just as I was opening my mouth to quiz him, a car horn went off outside loudly just below the window. I stared in astonishment at Arthur as he twinkled back at me. "You don't have the monopoly on excitement you know." The horn went off again and Arthur stepped across to look out of the window, leaving me standing with my mouth gaping, like a fish out of water. "Now who on earth is that outside?" he muttered. "Nice car, I must say." He opened the window to get a better look. "Oh."

"Oh what?" I asked, still glued to the spot. I was torn between wanting to know all of Arthur's secrets and never wanting to think about it ever again.

"I think someone's here for you, Jemimah." I walked over to the window and leaned out, as Arthur stood back and grinned at me. Tristan had heard the commotion and scooted in to peer through the window next to me. We both gazed down at the very beautiful black Bentley that was parked with complete disregard for legalities on the pavement outside the Mercury offices. Leaning against it and peering up with a hopeful grin underneath aviator shades, was Marc.

"I thought I'd give you a lift," he called up. When I didn't respond, Arthur gave me a sharp dig in the ribs.

"Go down and speak to the poor boy before he gets a ticket," he instructed sharply. Grabbing my bag and ignoring the curiosity of everyone in the office, I ran down the stairs, slowing near the bottom in order to not look quite as desperately keen as I felt.

As I pushed through the door, Marc loped over. "Thank you for looking after me," he said. Without warning, he leant over and hugged me. I held him tightly, not noticing that we were gathering an audience.

"Marc Gatton?" We reluctantly broke apart and turned to look at the young girl who'd spoken. She stood nervously, holding a pen out towards him. "Could I have your autograph?" Marc laughed. Putting an arm around me, he pulled me close whilst signing the girl's scrap of paper with the other hand.

Her friend took photos but Marc didn't make any move to hide or pull away from me. Turning to kiss the side of my face, he said, "Could you put up with me, do you think?" I looked him carefully up and down. He must have got a lift out to Heather's to collect the car and had clearly taken the time to bathe and change. He was dressed entirely in black from his t-shirt down to his boots and looked like a fallen angel.

"That depends," I said. "Where do you want to go?" Marc dangled my door key in the air, and then clasped it back in his hand with a grin.

"Let's go home."

THE END

And they all lived happily every after—or did they? Find out in part 2 of the Wonderland series: **Need You Tonight** is published Sept '22.

To keep up to date with new releases and preorders, gossip and background info on the world of Wonderland, **sign up for my mailing list**.

About Lily Farrell

Lily Farrell lives in Shrewsbury, UK with a ridiculous amount of pets and way too much beautiful-yet-ultimately-pointless clutter. She firmly believes that love conquers all (eventually) and that it's the baddest boys who often turn out to be the nicest.

To keep up to date with new releases and book gossip, join Lily's mailing list: https://bit.ly/lilyfarrell

Printed in Great Britain
by Amazon

18660237R00140